---◆---

Praise for Sheila Kohler

"Sheila Kohler's timeless stories are always transporting. The elegance of her writing underscores the charged, disturbing behavior she presents so vividly." —Amy Hempel

"A real master of narrative." —*Kirkus Reviews*

"Her themes of displacement and alienation cut to the heart as she quietly strips away the tales we tell ourselves in order to go on from day to day." —*Booklist*

Praise for
Love Child

"A widowed South African woman of forty-eight confronts the betrayals of her past in Kohler's graceful new novel. . . . Kohler's tale is full of tension, haunting images, and admirable restraint."
—*Publishers Weekly*

"[In a] sharply detailed book, [Kohler] portrays a slightly disreputable white woman in Johannesburg who came of age, married, had children, and was widowed, all within the confines of South Africa's English enclave. . . . Bill looks back and questions the choices that were made for her . . . A strong portrait of a weak woman. Recommend this to readers of Damon Galgut and J. M. Coetzee. For all literary fiction collections."
—*Library Journal*

"Secrets drive this gripping historical novel about a white South African woman. . . . mystery is always there. . . . Everyone compromises in this melancholy tale of looking the other way, and what holds the reader is how even the few dramatic revelations tell 'so little of the truth,' offering only haunting questions about the hidden power of money and prejudice."
—*Booklist*

"A woman's life of disappointment has been written thousands of ways, but the stories that endure dismantle the facades that time and practice erect over a lifetime of hurt and lost love."
—*The Washington Post*

"This novel packs a lot of story into its pages. . . . *Love Child* is an intriguingly messy story with an unusual perspective on family dysfunction."
—*ShelfAwareness.com*

"This story, set in the South Africa of the past, is the tale of a woman's revenge on her demanding husband and the privileged class she has married into—and the vindication of her secret past. Sheila Kohler's prose smokes and burns like a fire that cannot be put out and that suddenly leaps into all-devouring flame. She has all the gifts of a natural storyteller—a passionate interest in human motives, an eidetic recall of period and place, and a sense of the shape of a tale unfolding in the fullness of time."

—Edmund White, author of *City Boy* and *Genet*

"Sheila Kohler possesses a gorgeous imagination. *Love Child* is a warm, moving and beautifully crafted story of passion and loss and redemption." —Patrick McGrath, author of *Trauma*

"Absorbing settings with exquisitely rendered prose; Kohler's *Love Child* is a classic story of forbidden love and past lives told in retrospect. . . . Readers in search of a summer page-turner suffused with passion and intrigue, *Love Child* is a story that will take you there, and back." —Redroom.com

Praise for
Becoming Jane Eyre

"Exquisite . . . A stirring exploration of the passions and resentments."
—*The Washington Post Book World*

"Sensitive, intelligent and engaging . . . Kohler offers an imaginative recreation of the woman who created this once-scandalous, now beloved classic." —*Kirkus Reviews* (starred review)

"Passionate . . . a novel that refuses to be distracted from the simple but sophisticated act of literary creation."   —*The Boston Globe*

"Sheila Kohler moves with assured ease between fiction and biography, between the inner life of Charlotte Brontë as she composes *Jane Eyre* and the comedy of professional rivalry among the three Brontë sisters."

—J. M. Coetzee, author of *Disgrace* and *Summertime*

"Sheila Kohler's imagination—deep and playful, always original—instinctively completes that of her elusive subject, Charlotte Brontë, with such intelligence and perception that we give ourselves over without hesitation."   —Susanna Moore, author of *In the Cut*

"An unforgettable journey enriched by a sympathetic understanding of the three Brontë sisters as well as their writing."

—Frances Kiernan, author of *The Last Mrs. Astor*

"Sheila Kohler speculates with great grace and insight upon the currents that run between a writer's work and a writer's life."

—Julia Leigh, author of *Disquiet*

"Bravo! I couldn't put it down and finished it in the depths of the night."

—Lyndall Gordon, author of *Charlotte Brontë: A Passionate Life*

"*Becoming Jane Eyre* is lush and filled with dark sensuality and the tension of unsaid things. The style is quite different from Charlotte Brontë's in *Jane Eyre*, yet the tone and imagery and spirit remain in the same realm. *Jane Eyre* is one of my favorite books and Sheila Kohler one of my favorite writers."

—Amy Tan, author of *The Joy Luck Club*

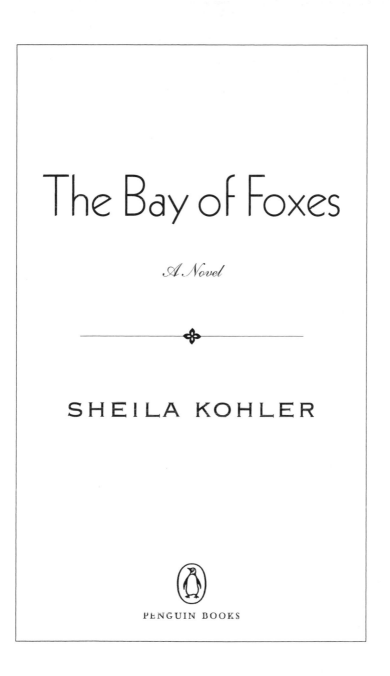

The Bay of Foxes

A Novel

SHEILA KOHLER

PENGUIN BOOKS

PENGUIN BOOKS
Published by the Penguin Group
Penguin Group (USA) Inc., 375 Hudson Street, New York, New York 10014, U.S.A. ·
Penguin Group (Canada), 90 Eglinton Avenue East, Suite 700, Toronto, Ontario,
Canada M4P 2Y3 (a division of Pearson Penguin Canada Inc.) · Penguin Books Ltd,
80 Strand, London WC2R 0RL, England · Penguin Ireland, 25 St Stephen's Green,
Dublin 2, Ireland (a division of Penguin Books Ltd) · Penguin Group (Australia),
250 Camberwell Road, Camberwell, Victoria 3124, Australia (a division of Pearson
Australia Group Pty Ltd) · Penguin Books India Pvt Ltd, 11 Community Centre,
Panchsheel Park, New Delhi - 110 017, India · Penguin Group (NZ), 67 Apollo Drive,
Rosedale, Auckland 0632, New Zealand (a division of Pearson New Zealand Ltd) ·
Penguin Books (South Africa) (Pty) Ltd, 24 Sturdee Avenue, Rosebank, Johannesburg
2196, South Africa

Penguin Books Ltd, Registered Offices:
80 Strand, London WC2R 0RL, England

First published in Penguin Books 2012

1   3   5   7   9   10   8   6   4   2

Copyright © Sheila Kohler, 2012
All rights reserved

Publisher's Note
This is a work of fiction. Names, characters, places, and incidents either
are the product of the author's imagination or are used fictitiously, and any
resemblance to actual persons, living or dead, business establishments, events,
or locales is entirely coincidental.

LIBRARY OF CONGRESS CATALOGING-IN-PUBLICATION DATA
Kohler, Sheila.
The bay of foxes : a novel / Sheila Kohler.
p. cm.
ISBN 978-0-14-312101-5
I. Title.
PR9369.3.K64B38 2012
823'.914—dc23   2012005999

Printed in the United States of America
Set in Bembo
Designed by Elke Sigal

For the immigrants, for the Africans,
and particularly for John, whose surname I never knew

For Nature, in no shallow surge
Against thee either sex may urge,
Why hast thou made us but in halves—
Co-relatives? This makes us slaves.

—HERMAN MELVILLE

The Bay of Foxes

PART ONE

---✦---

Paris

I

DAWIT IS SITTING AT THE BACK OF THE CAFÉ IN THE SHADOWS, when he notices her. She floats in from the street, her cigarette, in the tortoiseshell cigarette holder, held in graceful, tapered fingers. A plume of smoke obscures her face, but he knows at once who she is: M. With a thrill he recognizes the ethereal presence of a celebrity whom he sincerely admires. He stares at her tall, slim silhouette. Beneath her hat her white hair shimmers around her pale face like a nimbus. The large expressive eyes gaze dreamily heavenward. The long Modigliani neck arches arrogantly. She turns her head and stares at him.

He averts his gaze, conscious of his ragged jeans, threadbare shirt, holes in his shoes. Exhausted, faint with hunger, he has slipped into the shadows at the back of this café, ordered the cheapest item on the menu, adding several lumps of sugar, and lingering long over his espresso, which only the French seem to condone.

St. Sulpice.

The still Parisian square shimmers before him, and for a moment he is afraid he might fall from his chair. He lifts his cup to his lips with trembling hands.

Sometimes he kneels in the pews in the church on the square for hours. He prays to his guardian angels and the saints of his childhood, Saint Michael and Saint Gabriel, asking for help—he wonders how Jesus knew to tell his followers to ask God for their daily bread. He thinks of his father, who loved Paris so much and first brought him here. He sees him in the white garment his father wore at home, which would fall from his shoulder from time to time, and which he would adjust. With his deep-set, dark eyes, his playful, ironic smile, the small, neat mustache, he always seemed to be laughing at Dawit. Or Dawit just wanders around the side aisles, staring at the dramatic Delacroix paintings, the man wrestling with an angel. Like his father, Dawit loves Delacroix, who he knows visited Africa.

The café, too, is deserted at this dead hour on a late spring Sunday afternoon. The Parisians in this elegant quartier have already fled the town on the weekend for their country houses, for the sea. The waiters stand about idly in their long white aprons, vacant-eyed, their arms dangling lifelessly. From time to time their gazes register his dark presence with what seems to him suspicion. The French often take him for an Arab, which doesn't help.

He watches M. as she, too, sits down at the back of the café not far from him. The few people turn their heads, stare, and whisper to their neighbors. She is at the height of her fame, recognized wherever she goes as a rock star or a famous actress, her new book already both the Prix Goncourt for 1978 and a best seller.

She smiles at him curiously from the corner where she sits. He cannot keep his gaze from her pale face. He feels obliged to answer her smile as one would a mirror.

The famous face is found on the covers of her many books, which have been translated into every language under the sun. Highly praised by the critics for their originality, their distinctive voice and style, her books are also popular.

He had read them as an adolescent. His father had given him a cluster, taking them down from the shelves of his library, handing him the books with their distinctive cream covers and the name of the great French publishing house, the Nouvelle Revue Francaise, the *nrf* scrolled elegantly below the title. "You must read these," he can still hear his father say. "I think you will like them."

What Dawit appreciated was the authority of the voice, the brevity, the omissions, and, in one of his favorites, the unusual love affair: a young Ethiopian landlord of wealth, elegance, and position and his little white concubine, the girl he buys and falls in love with "to the death."

Dawit's father was a reader, educated abroad, first in England in exile with the Emperor during the Italian occupation, and later at the Faculté de Droit in Paris, where he did his law degree. Even his mother, from a family of priests, was sent to Switzerland to study French during the exile. His father had written a book on Ethiopian history. The family spoke both French and English, as well as an elegant Amharic, replete with multilayered puns and allusions. Dawit, taught by Orthodox priests, had learned to recite all the psalms in Ge'ez by the age of six. At ten, thanks to the Emperor, he had been sent to boarding school in Switzerland. At dinner the conversation sparkled, often in French or English so that the servants could not understand. The paranoia of the palace.

Now he glances warily at M.

She is wearing a mauve hat, which suits her, hiding what he surmises may be fine hair. The hat, despite its color, is mannish, with a wide brim, tilted slightly to one side, so that it shades her pale face. Her tailored, elegant clothes have a masculine air, too: the wide-legged gray linen pantsuit with the cream padded jacket, the striped gray and cream chiffon scarf, and the flat black tasseled shoes. He supposes they come from the Italian designer shop he has noticed on the square. She is smoking a Gitane in a tortoiseshell cigarette holder. She orders a *menthe verte*. She has a paperback book before her, but she is not reading. She is still staring at him.

Knowing something about her life from her books, he can imagine why. He was a reader and a writer at an early age. For years he kept a diary, writing ten pages a day in French or English, trying out different voices, different styles, looking for his own. He imitated M.'s spare, strong voice as so many did, the sort of distinctive style that enters the mind and echoes there, recording the events of life in her voice.

She is that rarest of writers, a literary best-selling one. Now, at her advanced age—she must surely be almost sixty—he finds her beautiful. She keeps looking at him as if she has seen him before.

He knows it is not just the glow in his smooth bronze skin that often seems to attract people, nor the high cheekbones, aquiline nose, large eyes, long, slender body, or even his youth. He is not yet twenty-one.

Mostly he dares not sit in expensive cafés. He walks the streets. He keeps moving for as long as he is able. He has no papers, no passport, no *carte de séjour*, not even an orange card for the bus. He hopes to mingle with the crowd, to hide, afraid of being followed, his own shadow, the police. He has seen what they do to African immigrants who attract their attention. His friend Asfa has told him of a man in the *banlieue* shot "by mistake." Every noise startles him, every glance causes panic, every word a death summons. He reproaches himself, hearing his father say, *They have turned you into a coward, Dawit!*

He has pawned the last of his mother's rings long ago. He owes Asfa money for the rent and food. He avoids him and the others in the crowded apartment, slipping down the stairs and out into the streets, ashamed to be seen in his increasingly ragged clothes, afraid to get caught up in endless and inconclusive conversations. Asfa would never press him for money, but Dawit knows his friend needs it badly. Asfa's own children are hungry, and his wife glances reproachfully at Dawit when she sees him.

He feels he has become invisible. People he knows shake hands with him so slowly and languidly and with such a bored expression, looking past him, he thinks they will fall asleep. Occasionally a stranger stops him, and he trembles, terrified. Usually it is a man whose gaze lingers on his shoulders, slender waist, narrow hips. He asks Dawit if he would like to come to his studio so that he could sculpt him, or something obvious of that sort. Dawit would like to ask if the visit would include a hearty meal, but he shakes his head, smiles, walks on.

Sometimes he does odd jobs if he can find them, but he is not strong. He has not been trained to do manual work. He has difficulty washing his own clothes. All through the winter he has had a constant cough from exposure to the elements. It has taken him a while to realize that the fine mist in the air is rain, that it will wet his clothes and skin. Besides, he has no umbrella or raincoat. He hugs the walls to stay out of the weather, a voice in his head recording his every step. Mostly, he thinks about food.

He has been hungry for so long now. At first he thought he would get used to it. Surely the stomach would adjust and shrink. But he has not. The hunger has become worse. Particularly as he walks past the bakery shops that trail their delicious scent of fresh bread, he is excruciatingly hungry. He has a craving for sweet things. He stands and stares at the croissants, the *pains au chocolat*, the *chaussons aux pommes*, as though he could absorb them with his eyes. He remembers the sticky deep-fried pastries of his childhood. Despite this longing he cannot manage to carry heavy things, the only work available.

Sometimes, despite the rain, the grayness, the hunger, despite the homesickness, he becomes aware of the beauty of the city, the quality of the flickering light between the leaves of the plane trees. He thinks of his mother lifting her lovely gaze to the light sky and saying, "*Levavi oculos,*" lift thine eyes, her Swiss school's motto. He thinks of the photo on her dressing table of her as a girl in her school uniform with the round felt hat, smiling shyly, showing uneven teeth, beside an identically dressed friend.

M. beckons him over now, waving her white hand, with its flash of square green emeralds. He approaches hesitantly, terrified but thrilled, not sure what she wants of him. She does not say anything but motions for him to sit by her in the wicker chair. She uses her lovely hands like a dancer, he thinks. He does not dare sit down—he can hardly breathe but just bends toward her.

Afterward, he is not sure why he says what he does. He has been brought up to be polite, to always be aware of how his words would be received, and he knows how important this might be, but somehow, despite himself, he hears himself telling her the truth, as one does an author whose books one knows so well.

"You have a ravaged face," he says, "but one which is more beautiful to me than it must have been when you were young and pretty." She smiles a little ruefully, as if acknowledging what has not been said, that the cause of her ravaged face is not only age. She must suspect he knows she is a drinker. She asks him to sit down beside her. "Tell me about yourself," she insists gently. Her voice has a deep, gravelly, masculine texture.

He perches on the edge of the wicker chair, ready to flee. Of course, he knows, or thinks he knows, how to respond to an invitation of this sort. He is careful what he says. He keeps his response short, underplays the recent events, and peppers it with a few exotic details. He makes some modest reference to his illustrious ancestors, his aristocratic family in Ethiopia, the privileged existence he led as an only child in the summer palace in Harar. He speaks of its surrounding scrub-covered hills, mild climate, stone walls, the guards at the gate, the chauffeur who drove his mother to the shops or to visit her friends, and that it was briefly the residence of Rimbaud.

He slips in a few intimate details about the Emperor:

the importance of protocol, the nine palaces, the coronation coach, the Emperor's formidable memory, of the necessity of gaining access to him, as his father, a minister of justice, was so skilled at doing, though even his father was banished for a time when he recused himself from a case in the sixties that he did not feel fit to judge; he talks of the importance of the Pillow Man, who slipped in the pillow so as to prevent any shameful dangling of the royal feet as the short Emperor sat on his high throne, the same pillow that slipped as easily over the Emperor's face, at the end, or so they said. He mentions the Purse Man, who doled out the envelopes that sometimes turned out to be empty or nearly so; the man called the Cuckoo Clock, who announced the passing of the hours.

He says something about the nationalization of his own family's lands. He says little about the student movement, the closing of the schools, the difficulties with the junta, the dreadful years of confinement, and the precipitous exit from his homeland with no more than the clothes on his back. He tells her he is a student of anthropology at the Sorbonne. He has occasionally managed to slip into an amphitheater and sit on a dusty step, trying to follow what some ancient man whom he could hardly see or hear was reading from a *polyco-pié*. He describes his homesickness, before returning to the subject of his admiration for her writing.

"You have described life in Africa so well," he says. He has seen one of the films for which she wrote the screenplay. She seems capable of going from book to screenplay without effort. He does admire her spare, concentrated prose, her brief, evocative novels, but he is also thinking of what she could do for him. He needs a place to hide, and he needs protection.

He is in constant fear the police will pick him up and send him home. Above all, he needs some peace of mind after the violence of more than two years in prison and the squalid life of his cramped quarters.

He can see she appreciates his compliments. "Where did you learn such excellent French?" she asks. He responds that he was given the traditional education of the children of Ethiopian aristocracy. His parents employed a French Capuchin monk to teach him the language, history, geography, philosophy, and Latin. His father admired the French, for supporting Ethiopia in its struggles against the British. Dawit learned English as well. He even speaks a little Italian. He has always been gifted at languages, has a good ear, indeed is musical. He plays the piano.

"Ah, the piano!" she says and opens her eyes wide. The bright light of her attention seems sincere, but he wonders if she really wants to hear about other people's lives. Perhaps his, coming from the Horn of Africa, where she, too, grew up, though under very different circumstances, is particularly interesting to her.

She speaks then longingly, as people do when they have lived in Africa as children, of the strength of the sunlight, something not to be found elsewhere, the warmth of the people, the friendly, easygoing way of life. "The light here seems diluted, like a weak glass of whiskey," she says, looking at him longingly, as though she might find the lost light in his bronze skin.

He says nothing about the terrible violence he has known, the brutality that contrasts with the beauty of the land. "October is the prettiest month," he says, remembering the fragrant yellow maskal flowers, which covered the fields in the spring.

What she remembers about Somalia are the women carrying pots on their heads, so erect that the pots seemed an extension of their bodies; the nomads in their long, sacklike robes, a large dagger at the belt; the camels, led so cruelly with a ring splitting their lips. She remembers their poverty, her mother suddenly washing all the floors and pouring water over her daughter's head, scrubbing her skin, then sending her daughter out to look for men. His presence seems to bring back her childhood, her dreams.

Her mother was a French teacher in French Somaliland. Her father died when she was four years old, leaving three children, two boys and a girl. She has known a life of extreme penury, eating garbage, or so she tells him. Her mother, a disturbed woman, used her as a prostitute, or close to that, before she could escape and return to France.

"I know what it's like to be poor and hungry," she says, looking at him with sympathy. He knows this story from her books. She returns to the same themes repeatedly: the death of her younger brother, the cruelty of the older one, her mother's madness, and her own African lover, a local landlord who must have been about Dawit's age now.

She looks him in the eye and leans toward him, so that her shoulder presses against his. She asks him about his religion. He tells her his father actually had little respect for the clergy, whom he considered ignorant and greedy, but his mother was devout. Her Coptic Christianity was very important to her, but despite the boarding school in Switzerland, she also worshipped the Tree of Life; there was room for both the saints and the *wukabi,* a pagan world within a modern one. "What a wonderful detail," she says. "I'll have to put it into a story." He suspects she makes people dance like this for her like puppets on a string, and then uses what they tell her in small, almost invisible brushstrokes in her many canvases. Writers are like vultures, picking over the tragedies of other lives, he thinks. But he can see that she wants more from him than recollections of a shared past. She leans toward him again, lowers her hoarse smoker's voice, and says, as if talking to herself, "You resemble him."

He looks at her inquiringly.

"The one I lost. The one I wrote about, the lost lover in my youth. He had the same light of hidden flowers in his skin," she says, quoting someone, perhaps herself, and putting her hand to his cheek.

It is then he feels a stab of desire. He remembers the scene in her book, where she meets a young man at the ferry crossing on the Blue Nile, in his linen suit, with his expensive automobile, his desire. He wants to possess M., this woman who sits beside him. She must see a flicker of this in his eyes or feel it as he reaches out to touch the back of her fine white hand, a breeze of a caress.

Then she leans even closer to him. He can see she is unable to resist. She almost touches his cheek with her nose as though she wishes to breathe him in. He thinks of his mother telling him of his father's infidelity. "Fresh bread, that's what he wants, fresh bread." He knows, too, this is a unique opportunity, one that is not likely to come his way again.

She says, "I know something about the methods of the junta. It's a miracle you survived." She puts her hand on his arm, strokes the scars, the burn marks, the scratches. He says, "Actually, I didn't." Part of him is lost forever, escaped to a great distance from him, like her lost lover.

All his family is gone, he explains: his father executed with the other ministers on Black Saturday in 1974; his mother dying sometime afterward of untended wounds in the Akaki Prison, where she was held with the other princesses, he tells her.

"I'm so sorry," she says.

Her tears and kindness bring a rush of tears to his own eyes, as kindness so often does. All the time he has walked the hard, indifferent pavements of Paris alone, hungry, and wet, distanced from himself, all the time he has lived in the crowded, slovenly apartment in Clichy-sous-Bois he has not wept. Now, with her fine fingers on the back of his wrist, her watery blue gaze lingering on his face, he loses control and bows his head. He does nothing to check his tears. He weeps, his shoulders shaking. She puts her arm around him, holds him tight.

"You must come to my apartment. I will take you in, but you must give me a few days to organize things. Come in the afternoon, three days from now," she says, taking out her black Montblanc pen and writing down her address on the white paper napkin before her, the ink spreading like a blue stain.

"I couldn't possibly accept your hospitality," he says, but she doesn't seem to hear him.

"It's an apartment near here, on the street that runs along

the edge of the Luxembourg Gardens—the Rue Guynemer," she says and gestures across the square and up the street. "It's the first floor. Just come up the stairs. Come after lunch. I'll be waiting for you."

Then she rises, floating off down the street, her fine linen clothes blown against her body, her scarf fluttering around her neck, as if she were swimming.

II

HE TAKES THE BUS BACK TO HIS SUBURB, CLICHY-SOUS-BOIS. His fingers in his jean pocket touch the wad of bills M. has left on the table, the napkin with the address which he has already memorized. It is dark now. He goes into the local supermarket near Asfa's apartment and buys lamb for stew, salad, spinach, and big bunches of black grapes. Then he stops at the bakery and gets several large loaves of crusty bread and, for the children, pastries. He hugs the parcels to his chest, going fast along the dangerous dark concrete walkway, past the endless rows of identical, anonymous buildings, smelling the wonderful scent of fresh French bread. He carries the food up the ill-lit stairs, because the elevator is broken. The walls are covered with graffiti and filth, and sounds of loud voices, arguments, and screams of children come from behind thin doors.

Three teenage boys and a plump girl with wild hair come running down the stairs past him. They brush against him rudely, on purpose it seems, so that he almost drops his precious bags. He huddles against the concrete wall and swears at them. They laugh loudly as they clatter down the stairwell. "*Salaud!*" one of them shouts, as the glass door bangs shut.

Breathless, he enters the open door on the fourth floor, the air redolent with the odor of coffee and incense. He almost falls over the small child, Takla, Asfa's youngest, who is crawling across the floor, crying. "Here, *mamush*," he says, taking a warm *pain au chocolat* from the bag and giving it to the little boy, who sits on the dusty floor, thin legs apart, chewing, smiling up at him, happy. He goes into the hot, grimy, windowless kitchen and puts his bags down on the chipped counter, with its cigarette stains and sticky surface. He takes out the lamb and opens the wrapping, as the women crowd around to see what he has brought, marveling at the abundance. The older ones still wear slippers and white scarves around their heads, as though they were about to step out into the streets of Addis.

Asfa's wife, Eleni, looks up from the coffee she is pounding with a mallet she brought all the way from Djibouti, tears in her eyes at this sight. She asks him if he has robbed a bank. He laughs and says there will be enough to eat for everyone tonight: they must cook all the lamb for dinner. She says she will serve it with her *berbere* sauce, and he rubs his hands at the thought of the spicy taste. He asks her if Asfa is home yet.

Before he left Addis Ababa, a friend had given him Asfa's address. Now Eleni scowls at him and tips back her shapely head to indicate her husband's whereabouts. She says he is there with yet another of his rescued victims. An unusually lively and good-hearted man, Asfa seems unable to turn anyone away, much to his poor wife's despair. In his great, openhearted generosity he seems almost simpleminded, which indeed his wife accuses him of being, though she knows he is not at all simple, having earned a degree in engineering from the university in Addis.

Dawit goes into the smoke-filled back bedroom to find

his friend. Asfa is watching a soccer game on the television. He sits cross-legged on a cushion on the floor with a group of young men crowded around him. There is hardly any furniture in the whole apartment except for the large television set, which always seems to be on. Asfa smiles broadly at him. He rises to his full height and strides across the floor through the others to greet Dawit enthusiastically, asking him where he has been hiding.

Asfa is the only one of these men who has managed to find a regular job. He works in a hotel in Paris, where he has to wear a ridiculous uniform, a long, braided coat with a high hat. He does all sorts of menial jobs, thanks to his great strength. He is remarkably tall and strong but subject to violent fits of rage and once felled a man with one blow. He leaves every morning before dawn to take the long bus ride into the city and often comes back late.

Now he asks Dawit why they have seen so little of him, why he has become such a stranger, why he leaves before anyone is up in the morning and comes back so late at night. Why does he no longer eat with them? In response Dawit looks at the scuffed linoleum on the floor, takes some of the money out of his pocket, and hands it over. "Here, take this. I'm sorry it is so little and so late," he says and presses it into his palm, while Asfa whistles and stares at the wad of bills suspiciously. He seems surprised and disconcerted. He frowns, shakes his head, and looks at Dawit worriedly. Dawit adds, "I hope to have the rest of what I owe you soon—perhaps more than that," as Asfa looks down at him in wonder. Asfa says, "Are you sure about this? There is no rush. We are happy to have you here with us, brother. You would do the same for me."

He speaks in a low voice, smiling at him but looking concerned by this sudden good fortune and putting an arm protectively around his shoulder.

He is too polite to ask the source of this good fortune, but clearly it troubles him. He mumbles something about money not having any real importance where friendship is concerned.

They eat sautéed spinach, salad, bread, and the stewed lamb, with the spicy sauce that brings tears to Dawit's eyes, all served on a large platter, which the women put down in the center of the table so that everyone can help themselves. They dip into the platter with their fingers and mop up the sauce with the bread. They drink cheap red wine, which Asfa brings out in honor of the meal and of what he calls Dawit's newfound fortune. No one questions Dawit about the source of the money, though they eye him suspiciously.

Clearly they cannot imagine such a sum of money appearing suddenly in a legitimate fashion. Asfa makes various circumlocutions about the value of integrity and the importance of freedom, and his wife tells him he talks too much. Dawit smiles but says nothing about his meeting with M., which is already beginning to seem like a dream. They all sit huddled around the kitchen table, talking and laughing over the stained linoleum cloth, while the children crawl around on the scuffed floor under the table. Everyone is delighted.

Dawit picks up the youngest boy, little Takla, who is crying again. The child seems to have difficulty catching his breath. Dawit dances him on his knee, and the child stops his wailing, but his breath still comes in small, desperate gasps. He looks up at Dawit with his enormous dark eyes, which look still larger in his pinched face. The little boy's only garment is a tattered shirt. Dawit wipes away the boy's tears with his paper napkin and wonders what will become of him in this strange, sunless country. He feeds the little boy from the big bunch of grapes, opening each one to extract the pips before passing it to him, watching the child savor the sweet black fruit with pleasure and ask for "More! More! More!" which seems to be the only word he knows. The very walls of this place seem to echo with his cry.

On his arrival here, Dawit had been shocked at the squalid, cramped quarters, these degrading conditions, with only one filthy, malodorous, and eternally overflowing toilet. When it was flushed, the water would jump up high and splash the user, if it functioned at all. It was impossible to wash properly without going to the public baths. The windows leaked, the rain seeping into the ill-lit, filthy hallways. What bothered him above all was the constant noise, the impossibility of a moment alone, a moment of silence. Now he has the possibility of leaving this sordid place behind, perhaps of helping his friends, as well.

Despite the copious meal he has eaten, for the first time in years he is unable to sleep that night in the cramped room he shares with the others who have found shelter here. They have so little space to sleep in they have to turn together. They are not much better than the people in the prison cells in his country that many of them have fled. He lies without a sheet over him, fully dressed, his small stock of underwear and clean socks, his few books, all his earthly goods bundled under his head for a pillow. Uncomfortably, he listens to the stertorous breathing of the others around him, the coughing, an occasional dream-cry in the night, and wonders if M. will really take him in, a strange Ethiopian. Will she reconsider and turn him away? He is afraid she may have been drunk, though she did not seem drunk to him. Had the *menthe verte* gone to her head? Perhaps she will have forgotten her encounter with him completely by the time he arrives? And if she lets him in, what will she expect of him in return? What is the quid pro quo here, and is it something he can provide?

III

_____

WHEN HE FINALLY FALLS ASLEEP, HE DREAMS A TERRIBLE dream. Often his dreams are so close to memories they wake him up, rather than allowing him to sleep. In this one he is back in prison. Perhaps because of his father's prominence, they had isolated him, and he had the privilege of being alone in his cell with the cockroaches and rats. There he had come to forget even the sound of his own voice, for though he chanted all the poetry he knew by heart, and all the psalms and prayers, and sang aloud the hymns, his voice came to him as if from someone else. He had the impression they had split him in two with their instruments: he was both Dawit and a stranger who lay curled up, weeping and beating his fists against the rough concrete wall. With the silence, the light that worked only randomly, and the ceiling so low he could not fully stand, they had reduced him to madness. Every sound terrified him: the screams and whispers from beyond his walls. With every footstep he was convinced someone was coming to take him to his death. Lions, hyenas, and jackals, snakes and spiders, lurked in the corner of his cell, ready to pounce on him and devour him.

He did not know how long he had been there, only that there was no way to distinguish one day from the next. There were no windows, and the lightbulb that hung in a net in the low ceiling went on and off according to the whims of the faulty electricity. The food and water, too, came sporadically and in varying quantities. Sometimes he slept, but mostly he lay there chanting all the poems he had ever learned.

There was a big, burly guard who particularly enjoyed tormenting him. He had noted differences among his torturers: there were those who carried out orders without any particular pleasure. But there were others who enjoyed the work and accomplished their tasks with particular inventiveness. They took an obvious pleasure in creating as much pain as possible. This guard was one of the latter. Probably he had been taught to think of Dawit as a corrupt and spoiled member of the ruling classes, an arrogant adolescent playing at politics in the student organization he had joined. The guard called him an "aristocratic anarchist" and mocked him for causing his own downfall. "An easy target," the guard told him, and laughed. It was a fertile line of reasoning. He had indeed been critical of the old regime. He had seen its abuses up close, the infighting, the promotion of people without talent, the graft. The guard had used all the usual means to induce him to betray his comrades, yet there was always a small part of Dawit that escaped, something that enabled him to remove himself to the mansion of his childhood, the cool, high-ceilinged rooms, the scented garden, his friend Solo's arms. Possibly the guard sensed this, and it spurred him on. Someone must have been determined to keep Dawit alive and in solitary confinement indefinitely, if he had not been lucky one afternoon. The miracle M. had spoken of in the café did occur.

A new guard opened the door and came in, sliding the rusted can with the dry bread and urine-tainted water across the cement floor. A beam of light entered the cell. Dawit's vision was blurred, and the edges of the pallet where he lay seeped into the hazy tips of the guard's stub-toed boots. It was the sharp creases of his new starched trousers, the sudden scent of lemongrass, the thick-meshed black eyelashes that brought it all back: the ragged but ironed shorts and the carefully stitched T-shirt, the long, slim limbs, the slight body disappearing fast into a loquat tree. Solomon. He almost said his nickname. Solo. He lifted his blurred gaze toward him— just a moment of communication, a stare that made the undulating lines in his world spin in the gust of clean air and light entering suddenly from beyond the cell walls.

For a moment he thought he was hallucinating, lying there, hands and legs attached to a heavy chain, his body nothing but bruised flesh and swollen joints.

Dawit had grown up with Solo, the son of one of the palace servants. All Dawit's childhood memories were inextricably linked to him. They had made slingshots together from elastic bands and wooden handles and hunted doves, cuckoos, and cranes at dusk in the freedom of that vast garden; they had climbed trees, picked loquats, half naked. They had hiked together in the hills around Harar, which they had been warned were dangerous. Solo had been his first love—there was no other word for it. He had never forgotten how Solo would come to him in the dark of night, slipping into his room and holding him fiercely, sleeping by his side, their limbs entwined.

Nor had Solo forgotten Dawit.

When the door closed again, Dawit pulled apart the lump of hard bread and was not surprised to find the sharp file. It took him hours and hours, shackled as he was, and constantly fearing someone might come to drag him out, as they did periodically, but eventually, desperation making him suddenly strong and persistent, he was able to free first his hands and then his ankles from their shackles. He stood partly up, for the first time in months without his chains, leaning against the wall and waiting for the door to open.

He is not really sure if he is dreaming or remembering, but he repeatedly replays the film of the moment the young guard came into his cell at dawn: he leans trembling against the wall, listening to the thick military boots stomping along the corridor; he sees himself behind the door as it swings open, holding the chain that had shackled him in his hands.

He had hoped it would be the guard who had tormented him so viciously, which as it turned out it was not. Perhaps it made no difference which guard it was at that moment. As with a sexual encounter, it is probably the first time that you remember best. He sees the guard's surprised stare as he catches sight of Dawit behind the door. There was no time to hesitate. He recalled the names of warriors his father had told him about, Aregay, Merid, Amaha, Alemayehou. He watches again and again, strangely distanced from himself, yet remembering how feeble he felt, his arms and his legs weak so that he could hardly stand, as he threw the chain around the guard's neck and pulled as hard as he could, suddenly filled with a rush of strength. He watched as the guard lifted his hands, searching desperately to free himself, gasping for breath, his eyes protruding from his flat face. He listened to the final throttled cry that came from the guard's swollen lips. At that moment Dawit was able to close his eyes and to conjure up all the rage he had stored in his wounded body over those months of helpless captivity. Every insult and indignity, every torment, was avenged in that moment of violence.

He held on for longer than was necessary or prudent, squeezing every bit of breath and life out of the body. The guard wore a khaki cap that fell back from his head, exposing his dark hair and black eyes. Then Dawit let the body slip down onto the cement floor, though he was not completely sure the guard was dead. He kicked him a couple of times in the groin, where they had put the electrodes that had made him jerk and burn and freeze at the same time, making his body split apart. He had recalled the old method of pulling a body apart with horses; this was more efficient; they had split his mind and body irreparably.

He pulled first the shirt and then the trousers from the guard's body. Quickly he pulled off his own filthy clothes and donned the starched, clean uniform, tucking in the shirt and pulling in the belt to hold the trousers up on his emaciated form. He angled the cap down over his eyes. He pulled on the heavy boots, loosened the keys from the belt, and made his way quietly down the narrow corridor, retracing the steps that had first led him there.

In his dream he sees the filthy, empty corridor with no sign of life, the same concrete walls. His knees almost buckle under him as he walks, and he puts his hands against the walls to steady himself. He glances around fearfully, but luck is with him: no one comes. He is tempted to unlock the five cell doors he passes on his right, where he sees no sign of light or life. He wants to free the other prisoners but realizes none of them would make their way to safety. Instead, fumbling, he finds the key to the door that leads into the courtyard and steps out into the first light of day. The other guards, crossing the courtyard, pay no attention to him. They came and went so frequently that a strange face could pass undetected. He is able to walk unhindered through the heavy door, out of the concrete building, into the dry patch of earth, the flat land all around. He makes way his way through the staring crowd at the entrance, all those relatives waiting for news of their loved ones. They are like shades in hell. He walks away from them, going through the parking lot with its military jeeps, trucks, and cars. He notices an old Volkswagen, where he sees three people sitting waiting in the dawn light. He goes down the narrow, dusty thread of a street that no longer seems real to him, finding his way. He takes off the cap and throws it onto the ground. He staggers onward. He is free: a rootless tree, an irremediably truncated tree, a tree without sustenance, but free nonetheless.

I V

THE MORNING AFTER HE MEETS M., HE GOES TO THE NEAREST
Monoprix, picking up and putting down various garments.
He chooses a tight-fitting black cotton shirt with long sleeves
and a round neck, and khaki trousers with pleats at the waist
that make him look a little less emaciated. He buys tooth-
paste, a comb, and soap. On the third day he goes to the public baths early and washes himself thoroughly. Then he takes
the bus back into the city.

He stands in the afternoon shadows of the chestnut trees
opposite M.'s blond stone building on the side of the Luxembourg Gardens. He looks up at the first floor and sees the terraces, the green plants in the window boxes, the red awnings.
It seems another world, as though he has stepped out of a
place of grayness into bright light.

He feels, as he did in prison, that he is split in two. He is
Dawit in his stiff new clothes in the uncertain light, and he
is watching himself, a young, painfully thin man with large
dark eyes. He is unable to move. His head spins, and he hears
the voice like an echo writing the novel of his life. His mind
is filled with words that record his actions, or rather his inca-
pacity to act. He has been alone for so long that this voice has
become his companion, the secret sharer of his destiny. He

must cross the street. He must ring the bell. He must ring the bell.

He forces himself to cross the street and press the shiny brass button that opens the door. He walks quickly past the concierge's loge with its net curtain, afraid she will stop him. He goes up the step and opens the glass door. He sees the small elevator, but M. has told him to come up the steps, so he runs up the shallow carpeted steps, two at a time. He stands in the unfamiliar silence to catch his breath on the landing. There seems to be only one apartment on each floor. He rings her doorbell. He waits in the silence. Just as he is beginning to lose hope, he hears steps, and she opens the door.

She is wearing blue jeans, flat shoes, and a white shirt, the sleeves turned up to the elbows. She has tied her white hair back from her face, which makes it look more pointed. She looks at him blankly, as if she does not quite remember who he is. He draws himself up and lifts his chin. "You told me to come this afternoon," he says. *Please don't turn me away*, he prays.

He has scrubbed himself, brushed his teeth, and tied back his unruly locks as best he could. He knows he needs a haircut. He has done the best he can with his appearance, but perhaps she has forgotten what he looks like, how dark his skin, or even how young he is, how thin? Perhaps she has forgotten the encounter altogether? Is it possible she was drunk? Does she regret her act of generosity? Does she wonder suddenly if he will steal her silver or put a knife in her back?

She tells him to come inside and shakes his hand solemnly in the large entrance hall, as though they were meeting for the first time. Her hand is icy cold. She has tied a small blue scarf stiffly around her long neck. He does not know what else to say, and she does not say anything. She does not offer him anything to eat or drink. Had they not talked about Africa, about the large families, the way people helped one another? Had she not put her arm around his shaking shoulders? Is she going to send him away? But she tells him to follow, turns and walks rapidly. They cross the shiny parquet floor, the sound of their shoes loud in his ears. They go through a *grand salon* with a black leather chaise longue and a fireplace at one end, a *petit salon* with a Louis XVI desk, soft blue and red Oriental rugs with animal designs, filled bookcases, and pink flowers fanned in glass vases. They walk through a formal dining room, with a silver bowl in the center of a long mahogany table. All these rooms look directly onto the Luxembourg Gardens and, across them, just visible through the first yellow-green leaves, the Panthéon. Even the kitchen looks through French windows onto a small terrace and the gardens.

They go down a dark, narrow corridor, where the rooms are much smaller and look over a courtyard, shadowy rooms once or perhaps still used for the staff. There is a little sink in the corridor, and closets that seem to go up to the ceiling.

At the end of the corridor, she pushes open a door. There is barely room for a single bed, with its dark green counterpane and an old frayed armchair with a small white towel over the arm, and to his surprise and delight, a battered upright piano with a candle-shaped lamp on top. She shows him at the end of the corridor a back entrance to the apartment, through which he can come and go as he wishes. She presses the key into the palm of his hand and tells him the room is his, as well as the small bathroom with a shower and toilet next door.

He can only thank her, bowing his head. She cuts short his thanks and says he is free to use the kitchen, too, during the day.

He steps into the room, walks over to the window, and looks down into the courtyard with the green dustbins, plants, and the entrance to the back staircase. Briefly he wonders who inhabited this room before him, and why she had asked him to come three days after they had met. Has he displaced someone? And if so, what has happened to him or her? He looks around, just as he had in his cell, to see if there were messages written on the walls, wondering if the previous prisoner had survived.

She leaves him "to settle in," she says, though he has nothing with him but a small plastic bag with a change of underwear, socks, a pair of shorts, and a few toiletries, which he lays out carefully by the basin, then stacks by the bed the three paperback books that he has picked up on the quay: a copy of Baudelaire's *Fleurs du mal*; Marguerite Duras's short stories, *Whole Days in the Trees*; and Dostoyevsky's *Crime and Punishment*.

Alone in the room, he puts the precious key in his pocket and shuts his door. He takes off his worn shoes and stretches out on the bed, opens up his arms, and stares at the ceiling, the voice in his head loudly recording all of this. He falls into a deep, dreamless sleep. When he wakes, he gets up and drinks some water from the basin in the corridor. Then he opens the piano, a German one, a Schimmel. He looks at the yellowed keys. He places his fingers on them, shuts his eyes, and feels his way, playing from memory the simple pieces from his childhood. He plays a Chopin étude, the notes coming back to him from the tips of his fingers where they have remained.

He remembers the music teacher who came to the mansion, a blond young man from Sweden—the Emperor liked Swedes—whom his mother was always trying to marry off but who was clearly not interested in women. The teacher would stand behind Dawit as he sat at the piano, and reach over his shoulder to press down on the keys and against his back. Dawit has not played for years. Slowly, the notes of the Chopin replace the voice in his head.

He hears a knock on his door and rises quickly to open it, conscious of the holes in his socks. To his surprise, M. is wearing a white dishcloth tied tightly around her small waist. She asks him if he would join her for a simple meal. "I would like to cook something for us," she says, almost shyly. He hesitates a moment, fearing that if he eats with her tonight, she will want him to do it every night, and he wonders what might be expected of him in repayment for the meal. But he is hungry, afraid of offending, and delighted with the small, quiet room with its piano. He smiles, nods his head, thanks her for her kindness, and puts on his shoes. He follows her into the kitchen. He asks her if there is something he can do to help, but she smiles and shakes her head. He sits on a stool and watches as she boils water in a big pot, washes the lettuce, and makes the dressing, dosing oil and vinegar judiciously, cutting the little loaf of bread.

"I hope this will be enough for you," she says, serving the small bowls of pasta with oil and anchovies. He could easily eat three times what she serves him and would like to ask for cheese, but he murmurs politely that it will more than suffice. They eat together in her kitchen, perched at a counter on high wooden stools awkwardly, like two caged birds, side by side. She eats very little, mostly sipping her drink. All their intimacy is transformed into awkwardness, now that he is alone with her in her house. He eats fast, distractedly, thinking of his last dinner with Asfa and his family, all the good-humored jokes, the children's laughter, little Takla on his lap.

As soon as he has finished, he rises, says the pasta was delicious, and thanks her for the meal. She takes the dishes to the sink and starts to wash them. He offers to help, but she tells him there is a dishwasher, and the concierge is coming in the morning.

He says he is very tired and must go to bed. She looks at him, tilts her head to one side, and tells him she is afraid he might still be hungry, but she never eats meat or touches sugar or cream. Instead, she confesses, she drinks. She likes gin or, most of all, vodka, and she pours herself another glass. Would he not like a drink? He declines.

When he leaves her to go back to his room, he notices she follows him and locks the door that leads to the large reception rooms of the apartment, where her own bedroom must lie.

V

HE NEED NOT HAVE WORRIED ABOUT THE INVITATIONS TO
dinner. She does not invite him to another one for several
days. Indeed, he hardly sees her. He comes and goes through
the back door, quietly, unseen, unheard.

He is an early riser, trained by the monks to say his prayers
at dawn. He slips down the back stairs at first light, the sky
still a faint pink. He likes to run. It reminds him of his childhood, when he would escape barefoot from the mansion,
running free into the hills around the town with Solomon,
though they had been warned about the hyenas and jackals in
the hills. Now he runs alone around the Luxembourg Gardens, barefoot on the blond footpath, as he did as a child, running fast, going past the white marble statues of queens long
since dead, staying within the high, gold-tipped fence. He is
still a good runner, even after the beatings and bruising of
his feet. The few people up at that hour watch him pass with
curiosity.

M., he gathers, is often just going to sleep. She seems to go
to sleep very late, but she opens the door so he can come into
the kitchen before she sleeps. She does not use the reception
rooms in the day. Perhaps she awakens late and works in her

wide bed in the afternoons and through the night, as he never sees her at her desk.

One afternoon, he catches a glimpse of her bedroom when the concierge leaves the door open. While the concierge, with her back to him, pushes the noisy vacuum cleaner, he peeps in. He sees M.'s manuscript spread all over the sheets, her old typewriter, an Olivetti, propped up on a board across the bed, cigarette stubs piled up in ashtrays, books and bottles scattered all over the floor. Despite the drinking, he decides, she must be an almost constant worker. Apparently no one is ever allowed to disturb her work. When she is working she does not go out, even to see her friends. She says, "I'm pulling down the veil," and she smiles and makes a gesture of pulling something down over her face, as their paths cross for a moment in the kitchen.

Not many people seem to call. The telephone rarely rings. Like him, she has no family left, she has told him, since her mother and both her brothers died long ago. Her younger brother, whom she loved dearly, died as a child. She must have good friends, or at least many acquaintances, fans, surely, but they seem to respect her privacy and perhaps wait for a summons from her. He realizes she must live the dead-quiet life of a working writer much of the time.

He would like to repay her kindness—he would like to contribute to his rent, he says, when he sees her in the kitchen, coming in one evening for a bottle of tonic water and ice from the refrigerator. She has been so kind. It is such a privilege to live near these beautiful gardens, in this safe and quiet district, above all to have the luxury of his own room. "I feel as if I have stepped from hell into paradise," he says quite truthfully. She smiles and says it is not necessary. He cannot accept charity, he says. She presses on, "It's so rare we have the opportunity to pay our debts, and I feel I have a debt to you and your people."

He goes to the shops with the little money he has left and looks for something to buy her. He recalls the market in Harar, the beggars pleading, goats bleating, the merchants elbowing their way forward to approach his nurse, crying out, "Lady, lady, real silk, Indian silk!"

All he can find is a large bunch of yellow daisies that make him think of his homeland, the maskal flowers. He puts them in a blue and white pitcher on the kitchen counter. When she comes into the kitchen, she thanks him for them, leaning over and smelling them as though they were roses.

He says he wishes he had learned to cook or to clean the house, but no one ever taught him how. Brought up with a household of servants, he is not very good at it. He remembers the elderly retainer, Yonas, who polished the silver to such a high shine, buffed the furniture, scrubbed the dishes, and polished the stone stairs in the palace with such diligence, half singing, half whistling.

She explains that the concierge, Maria, comes three times a week to clean and cook. She is Portuguese, an ungainly young woman with big feet and red hands, and she weeps a lot. He notices that she seems to be pregnant. She has an open, kind face and cleans thoroughly and cooks delicious soups and compote to last the week. She startles easily and jumps each time he appears. "I'm not dangerous, I promise," he tells her with a grin, and she smiles at him and bobs her head.

"*Bien sûr, monsieur,*" she says, but she continues to startle at his presence.

When she falls sick for a few days, M. cooks him a dinner of fried fish, which she picks at politely, leaving most of it on the serving platter. Afterward, he thinks he would like to take what remains to Asfa's family. Instead, on an impulse, he carries the platter down the stairs and knocks on the concierge's door. She opens it in her pale gown, her eyes red. "I brought you some dinner," he says. "Monsieur is too kind," she says and grins broadly, her pale cheeks flushing with pleasure.

Mostly, M. tells him to help himself from the cupboard and goes back into her room. He eats what she leaves in the refrigerator: little dishes of steamed spinach and salad, leftover pasta with fish, bread, but sometimes after dinner he goes for a stroll and buys a bar of chocolate with the small store of money he has left. He eats it ravenously in his room.

"Good," she says, looking at him one evening when she sees him in the hall. "You are putting on weight, filling out, and I don't hear you coughing as much." Though he thinks of Hansel and Gretel in the witch's house being fattened up, he only says, "I am happy here."

VI

SHE HAS BEEN OUT THIS AFTERNOON AND RETURNS CARRYING big, shiny packets from the fancy Italian store on the square. He is standing on the little terrace at the window with one foot in the kitchen and one outside in the sunlight, looking over the gardens, eating a piece of bread and jam for his lunch. He recalls his days as a boy in the palace gardens in Harar, the freedom of climbing trees, of escaping on hikes into the hills. He and Solo were reckless, unafraid of the hyenas that roamed the hills around the town or even the people in the summer palace whose intrigues and maneuverings they watched with interest, secure in the shadow of his father's position and the Emperor's protection, which seemed unlimited, unassailable, God-given. All that has been shattered utterly, and he is terrified of everything. He stays close to the apartment on the Rue Guynemer as though its luxury could protect him from the dangers that proliferate outside. He has not been back to his *banlieue*.

It is past noon, and the sun comes and goes behind clouds— a French day, two weeks since he arrived. He is still wearing the same shirt and the khaki pants from Monoprix, which he has washed by hand in the basin and hung out in the sunlight on his balcony to dry. She looks at him as she puts her purple packages down on the counter. She lifts the tips of her two middle fingers to her lips, considering something.

"Come with me," she says and takes him by the wrist, leading him into her big bedroom with the queen-sized bed and its shiny green brocade counterpane. Her bedroom, like his, looks over the quiet courtyard with its plants, dustbins, and back staircase. The room has stained-glass windows, as if in a church. "It used to be the dining room," she says, as though that explained the windows.

She leads him into an enormous bathroom with dark brown wall-to-wall carpet. Against one wall are a huge tub, a mirror, and green wallpaper with a jungle pattern above the mirror. On the opposite wall is a row of closets. She throws open the double doors on a walk-in closet. There is a mirror against the back wall, so you can see front and back.

"Let me see what I've got here that might do," she says, turning her head, studying him. "You need some clothes." He stares at the racks of designer clothes, pantsuits, a few long evening dresses in dark colors, stacks of cashmere sweaters, linen shirts in all the colors of the rainbow, and below in the shoe racks all the polished shoes with their shoe trees. Mostly she wears flat shoes, because of her height, he presumes.

She is the same height as he, nearly six feet, though much frailer. She is very thin. She has no hips, and her legs are like brittle twigs. He has already noticed that she is very careful what she eats. He surmises she may have an eating disorder, or perhaps it is all the alcohol she drinks that takes away her appetite and gives her such thin legs.

He, too, is thin. He was always so, much to his mother's

dismay, and his years in prison, the dreadful voyage to the coast in the back of a covered truck and then on the ship from Djibouti to France, the penury of his life in Paris for several months have reduced him to no more than skin and bones. For months he has not had a proper meal, subsisting on stale bread and an occasional piece of fruit or vegetable stolen from an open stand.

She pulls down heaps of sweaters and pushes them into his arms. She takes jackets off hangers, shirts, hands him shoes. She says, "I have to buy my shoes in America—size eleven—or I buy men's sizes." He just looks at her.

"Try them on," she commands.

He puts the clothes down on the shelf and hesitates, watching himself in the mirror. "Go on," she says, hovering behind him, not making any move to leave him alone to undress. He pulls his T-shirt over his head. He is plunged into darkness for a moment before he emerges into the bright light, where he can count his ribs, which seem to try to thrust their way out of his skin. Quickly he pulls on a soft black turtleneck sweater. He puts a jacket over it. The sleeves are a little short when he stretches out his long arms, but otherwise it fits. He stares at his reflection in the mirror before him. The jacket acquires elegance, a fine line, the allure of his youth. Also, there is grace in his long neck and the tilt of his head.

"Try these," she commands, giving him a pair of linen trousers.

He hesitates again, thinking of his threadbare and possibly stained underwear. "Don't be ridiculous," she says. He is obliged to take off his khaki trousers and quickly pull up her

Italian designer pants on his long legs. She gives him a leather belt to pull in the waist, so that they fit perfectly.

"It's amazing, we are the same size," she says, amused, looking at him in the mirror. She says, "A very young and dark double." Then he slips on a pair of long, narrow American shoes. He flexes his toes in the soft leather. They, too, fit. He needs new shoes. He can feel the earth through the holes when he walks in his lone pair. How he wants them! She has so many, all with their shoe trees. He stands before the mirror staring at his reflection, laughing at himself, at her hovering behind him, his young, dark head blooming where her old, pale one has wilted.

"*Formidable!*" she says and claps her hands. "*Magnifique!*" she says, thoroughly enchanted by his appearance in her clothes, as though she were responsible for it, with all his beauty, his life.

Indeed, he feels she has brought him back to life.

"You definitely look better than I do in these," she says, taking more clothes from the shelves, giving him another heap of sweaters, scarves, and even long-fingered leather gloves that fit perfectly. He stands there grinning in her gloves, with his arms filled with her designer clothes. Finally she takes a broad-brimmed black hat from the top shelf and angles it on his head. She stands back and admires, cocking her head to one side. The hat gives him a rakish air that reminds him of what he looked like as a young teenager, before all the troubles began.

How pleased he had been with himself in those days, he thinks with wonder, remembering standing in front of a mirror and flexing his muscles, an adored, pampered only boy who thought himself invincible, immortal.

"Perfect!" she exclaims.

"I can't," he says, taking off the hat, thrusting the clothes back into her arms. "I can't take your clothes. I can't accept all of this!"

"Go on, please. It gives me so much pleasure," and she gives him a soft kiss on the cheek, thrusting her things back into his arms.

"Then you must let me work for you. It would give me great pleasure," he says.

VII

HE AWAKENS IN HIS NARROW ROOM WITH A START, THE LIGHT in his eyes. He trembles with fear, remembering the light in the net in the center of the cement ceiling in the prison, which came on suddenly. "Please turn off the light! Please turn off the light!" he would plead with the walls, kneeling and putting his hands over his eyes. He craved sleep, oblivion. Sometimes he thought they had forgotten him there, left him alone to rot like carrion.

Then he realizes she is standing beside his bed. She has switched on the small candle-shaped lamp on the top of the upright piano to watch him sleep. It is hot in the airless room in the June night, though he had opened his window before he went to sleep and thrown the sheet back. Now he pulls up the sheet to his chin to cover his nakedness. He does not possess pajamas. He sits up, shaking.

"Don't be frightened. I'm just looking at you," she says, smiling, reaching over, and putting her hand on his arm.

"I wasn't frightened, just surprised," he feels obliged to say, though he is still trembling. Her face is pale without her makeup, and she is wearing a diaphanous black nightgown, her white hair loose around her face and shoulders, her slack breasts almost visible. She says extravagantly, "You are so beautiful, I would like to kill you. I will give you money, if you will make love to me."

He looks back at her, and she reaches out to stroke his cheek. He shakes his head, crosses his arms, and says, "I can't— that's all I can say. I just can't. If I forced myself, it would not be good for either of us. It might even be dangerous."

But she looks so sad, standing beside the bed on the small red carpet, and she is not asking for anything now, her shoulders slumped, her forehead down. He understands her despair. He understands desire. He says, "Turn off the light." She turns to do it. Then he hears her come back and sit down on the floor, close beside him in the darkness.

Naked, he gets out of his bed and squats beside her. In the narrow dark space, the two of them pressed together like children playing hide-and-seek, he reaches out for her. He feels for her face and shoulders. He lifts her black nightgown over her head. He thinks of the tall young lover, the elegant landlord, the one with the fancy car, the linen suit, the glittering rings, the one she lost long ago, or the one she imagined she lost, who picked her up on the ferry and took her back to the hotel room with its sounds of the street and the night. He wonders if there was ever a man who even vaguely resembled the handsome one she described so vividly, so entrancingly, in her book.

He lets his hands run down her long neck. She puts her hands on his shoulders and runs them down his smooth bare chest, while he touches her small, slack breasts, sunken stomach, bony hips. Her fingers are groping for his flaccid sex. Blindly he forces himself to move his hands over her body, the voice like a Greek chorus on a stage recording his actions. *He touches her legs; he runs his hands all the way down to the soles of her feet.* She moans softly in the heat of the summer night. He slips down, lying stretched out on the floor. He pulls her back. She is stretched out beside him in the narrow space. He feels between her thin legs. He touches her damp sex with horror.

He turns her body over quickly, unable to bear the rise and fall of her flesh, her dampness, her smell. He plants her down with a rough shove and a smack, pushes her face into the carpet cruelly. She groans. He feels the wings of her shoulder blades, straddles her body, and tries to enter her from behind.

"It's impossible," he says, getting up, turning on the light, standing over her. She goes on lying there before him, so thin and white, her hair on her shoulders, not moving, as if she were dead. She makes him think of the witch in the folktales his mother would tell him. When she turns onto her back and shields her eyes with her hands, she asks, "You could never desire me?"

He sits down on the edge of the bed, takes her hand, lifts her up, and makes her sit beside him. He says, "I think you are very beautiful."

She looks at him so sadly, tears shining in her eyes.

He recalls the moment when she told him about her lost lover. "That first day in the café, I wanted you, I really did. I remembered that beautiful description of the ferry on the Blue Nile, the African light glinting on the water, the elegant, dark young man. It was a book I read when I was young—I had never read anything quite like that, and I have always remembered that scene. Later I saw it, too, in a film. I don't know who played the role but I wanted *him*, the man in the white linen suit."

"Have you never desired a woman?" she asks.

"Never," he says, shaking his head.

"It seems inconceivable," she says. "Surely there must have been a moment, someone, sometime? Even your mother, when you were very young?"

He sits on the bed beside her in the hot, dark room and thinks of his mother finding him one morning with Solomon in his bed. She had taken him into her study, sat him down on her blue chintz-covered chair. She told him that these things happened in adolescence. She had felt the same way about a girl in her boarding school. She thought she was in love, had held her in her arms, but she had grown out of it. She had gone on to love his father so much, to have so much pleasure with him. "We change as we get older," she told him. He must not be ashamed, she said. She kissed him and told him that in any case she would love him, whatever happened, that he was her beautiful, beautiful boy.

Then she advised him not to say anything to his father. "Men, even sophisticated ones like your father, don't always understand these things. They see the world in black and white. We women understand that things are not as simple as they might seem," she had said. She added, "Your father, despite all his fancy degrees, was brought up to think of Ethiopian men as soldiers, and to consider valor in battle the ultimate aim for a man."

Now he leans back against the wall, his chest bare, and shakes his head, conceding, "Only you—for that second in the café."

"It sounds like a song," she says, laughing at him, singing in English now, "Only youooo!"

"Would you prefer that I go?" he asks, folding his fingers together in a position of prayer.

"No!" she says quickly. "If you stay with me I would be so glad; I would like you to stay very much. I feel as if I have found part of myself again, part of my youth." She holds his hands gently in hers.

"I so much want to stay," he says and turns his gaze away, so that she will not see his desperation, his need for her help. She adds something that reassures him, as it is intended to do, though he is not sure he believes her. She says casually, shrugging her narrow shoulders and in her deep, hoarse smoker's voice, "After a certain age, what women are looking for most is companionship and tenderness."

She tells him she is leaving for her villa in Italy soon, as she does every summer, and sometimes stays through the fall. Would he like to come with her? "The house is on the side of a steep hill with a beautiful view of the bay, Cala di Volpe. There is a little motorboat, islands, clear, clear sea."

"Cala di Volpe? The bay of the fox? Is that what it means?"

"You speak Italian, too?" she asks.

"A little." He has learned some from one of the Italian workmen who had remained after the brief occupation and worked in the summer palace. "Where is it?" he asks, intrigued, thinking of the Blue Nile, of the waters of Lake Tana and the monasteries his mother took him to visit as a boy. He was not allowed to swim in the lake because of the bilharzia, a parasitic disease in which worms enter the veins and feed on the blood cells.

"That's it. The Bay of Foxes. There are still some there. Also wild boar, which they hunt in the fall. We drive from here to Genova and take a ferry from there to the island of Sardinia. It's a beautiful island, still quite wild. D. H. Lawrence wrote about it. It has a wonderful smell—they say sailors passing in the night near their island can recognize it by its smell. I don't know what it is, some sort of herb, perhaps. Do you drive?" she asks him.

"That I *can* do. I love to drive," he says with a smile.

"Then you will drive my Jaguar," she says and adds, laughing, "A white one, a convertible."

"I don't have a proper visa, papers," he says, looking down at his hands, which he presses together.

"We'll get you the papers you need. I know the right people. Sometimes fame is useful. And in the winter you'll come with me to my chalet in Gstaad, will you?" she asks and reaches out again to touch his hands with both of hers.

"I will do anything I can to help," he says and looks at her directly.

"Just rest now here on me," she says and lies down on the bed. She parts her legs. He lays his head in the chink, his face against her sex. He lies there meekly. He can hear the sounds of the concierge coming into the courtyard to drag out the dustbins at dawn. She asks him to do it to her with his mouth, and he does, he does what she wishes him to do with his hands, his mouth.

VIII

She leaves the door open now so that he can enter the kitchen in the morning early, make his coffee, grill toast, boil eggs, if he wishes. She gives him work to do for her.

He spends long hours every day at her Louis XVI desk, which faces the gardens. From time to time he lifts his gaze to the light in the leaves of the chestnut trees. It is hard to believe he is here. For so long he stared at concrete walls. He feels he has been in a series of barely concealed coffins: the cement walls in the prison, the back of the truck with the tarpaulin hiding him, and the dark hold of the boat; the crowded bedroom in Clichy-sous-Bois. On the desk is a pretty blue glass flute filled with a bouquet of black Montblanc pens, a small African Venus with a big belly, a roll of stamps, and a black telephone. He moves his hands over these things as he reads.

She asks him to read books for her that people send her to review, to blurb, or just to read. "Say something kind that sounds generous but not stupid," she tells him with a smile. He is happy to oblige. He is a fast reader and can turn a phrase to advantage. About a book he does not understand at all, he says, "The author expresses all our bewilderment before the world."

"I see you are the perfect diplomat," M. says, standing over him, putting her hand on his shoulder, smiling down at him.

"I was brought up by diplomats. They trained me well. I learned the tricks of the trade," he says, grinning. He tells her how important it was to have access to the Emperor's ear in order to advance. The Emperor, with his excellent memory as well as his paranoia, played one faction against another. He held all the strands of the state in his hands. One had to learn to appear perfectly sincere in one's admiration. Dawit's father had indeed admired the Emperor's skill at creating a myth around himself, but he had used that admiration to advance his own career. He was a skilled courtier, a bon vivant, and a Francophile who liked women and wine.

Dawit answers her many fan letters, too. "Just say a few words, thank them for their kind thoughts, and sign my name," she tells him. He writes the kind of letters he would have liked to receive from her. He tells her fans how much their opinion matters, how much it is appreciated, how much it pleases her that someone far away has understood what she has tried to say. She reads a few of his letters. "Beautiful! You do this much better than I do!" she says. "You are an excellent scribe!" He practices the famous signature over and over, signing her name with a flourish.

She reads to him in the cool evenings before dinner as he lies on the black leather daybed with the doors open onto the terraces, staring out at the emerging stars. She reads what she has written during the night before, sometimes just a paragraph, sometimes several pages. He listens carefully. He knows how to concentrate. He responds without flattery. In the morning he pores over her manuscript, edits her sentences, leaves comments in the margins.

"I see you can be an honest critic, if you want to," she says, looking at him. "Thank you. It's rare, a precious gift."

She drifts into the study one rainy afternoon in her wide gray linen trousers. She is carrying an armful of unopened envelopes she has scooped up from beside her bed. "Can you sort these out?" she asks him, dropping the heap of letters onto the desk. They are from her bank, from magazines, newspapers, and her agent.

He has a good memory and a facility with figures. He knows how to read a balance sheet. He arranges her bank statements in chronological order. He sorts out the incoming checks, which tumble out of many envelopes. He balances her checkbook. He writes down sums in long columns. "So many of them!" he says, showing her the high pile he has made by that evening when she emerges with her drink.

"Let me sign a few over to you. You work so hard," she says, coming over to the desk, putting down her drink, plucking a pen from the blue vase. "I forget about them half the time."

"If you really want to give me money, I would prefer a monthly sum sent to an account in my name on a regular basis. Something small," he says, looking up at her.

"Of course," she says. "We'll go to the bank tomorrow, first thing," and they do go, though in the afternoon. Together they walk up the road to the Société Générale on the Rue d'Assas. She introduces him to the manager, an elderly gentleman in an elegant gray suit who ushers them into his office. She leans forward and tells him she wants to open an account for this young man. The bank manager smiles at him graciously from behind his wide desk, bowing his head and murmuring, "*Oui, bien sûr, avec plaisir, monsieur, bien sûr, monsieur.*" She arranges something generous to be deposited monthly to his account. He is given a checkbook, for the first time in his young life.

The first check he writes is for Asfa. He sends it to the apartment in Clichy-sous-Bois with a note with his thanks for taking him in, feeding him, giving him a place to sleep. He tells him to give little Takla a kiss and buy him some new clothes. He promises to come and see them all, but he does not. He does not take the long bus ride to the dangerous *banlieue*. Though he feels ashamed, he cannot bring himself to leave the comfortable *sixième*, where he is beginning to feel safe in his elegant clothes, shiny shoes, and affluence as he walks through the orderly streets. Nor does he write his return address on the letter.

Instead, he goes to the *boulangerie* and buys himself three *pains au chocolat*, and eats one after the other on the spot, as though someone might take them from him if he walked out into the street. He buys a big tin of sweets, too, which he hides under his bed in his room.

Then he sits down on a rented iron chair in the Gardens in the sunshine, all through the afternoon. Fascinated, he watches the grave French children in their long white socks and long smocked dresses, their knickers and shirts, being led back and forth, their little feet sticking out in their lace-up shoes, sitting on fat donkeys. The following Sunday, he stands on a corner and observes the smartly dressed couples with their small children, the father bearing a big bouquet of flow-

ers for the grandparents, perhaps. The order of French bour-
geois life is like a balm, though he studies it from a lonely
distance.

He establishes a routine. Every morning he rises early,
runs, buys a croissant and a café au lait from the café on the
corner, and then returns to work at M.'s desk. He opens her
mail for her, answers it, takes out the books she is sent.

There are packets from her agent, who sends M. her books
in translation. "What language is this?" he asks M., taking a
book out of a packet, lifting it up.

"No idea," she says and laughs. "I can't even remember
which book it is."

He writes thank-you letters to her agent, signs her name.

She asks him to answer the phone for her, too. An answering service is so impersonal, she says, no one should have
to talk to a recorded voice on the phone, and she doesn't want
to be disturbed. "Just say you are me and say something polite," she says. "You're such a diplomat and a good actor. You
sound just like me, anyway," she says, grinning at him with
amusement, listening to him speak with her hoarse, trembling man's voice, saying, "Allo," as she does, followed by
polite things. He does not find it very difficult. He has already
imitated her style as a teenager, writing in his diary. "How
lovely to hear from you. I've been thinking about you, darling, and wondering how you were," he says, leaning back in
her Queen Anne armchair with its pink silk covering, putting
his arms on the wooden armrests. He stares out at the leaves
on the chestnut trees, which hang down like ripe fruit ready
to be plucked. They remind him of the mango trees in the
garden of his childhood.

"You do that perfectly. You could fool my mother! If she were alive," she says.

Generally, he takes care of all the mundane details of her life, leaving her free to write, like so many literary couples before them. He considers himself naturally easygoing, pliable up to a point. He aims to please. He is used to trying to ingratiate himself, to question, to listen, and to give good advice. He was an only child who was often in the company of intelligent adults, courtiers in the various palaces of the Emperor or on trips abroad. He learned at an early age what to say to please his sophisticated father, who had loved him in a distracted, distant way, and how to calm his mother's constant anxiety. Only Solo, though older, followed him around the palace gardens and into the hills. Only Solo deferred to him completely, obeying his every wish.

Dawit adapts to M.'s schedule, her way of life. He listens to her, gives her good advice, and makes himself available to her. But there is a part of him she never reaches, a secret part that watches her with ironic detachment. Mentally he takes notes on the movements of her fine hands, her every expression, her particular words. He speaks her language perfectly, but she does not know a word of his. Despite her upbringing in Somalia, she has never taken the trouble to learn any of the languages of the country, he notes. He comes to know all about her intimate life, her work, her desires, but she knows very little about him. Like all colonizers, he thinks, she is ultimately the dupe.

"I WANT YOU TO COME WITH ME THIS EVENING, SO THAT I CAN introduce you," she says. She is sitting before her kidney-shaped dressing table with its sea green organdy skirt. She wears her silk dressing gown and brushes her long hair with a silver-backed brush. He comes over to her, takes it from her hand, and goes on brushing, as he did for his mother in her bedroom, where she kept the photo of herself in her school-girl uniform and her round felt hat on the table by her bed.

"You must wear something elegant," she tells him, look-ing at him behind her in the mirror. "Wear that black Armani pantsuit of mine with the hand stitching."

"Is it someone important?" he asks.

"Very important to me: my editor and his wife. I've known him for a long time. He's been good to me, published many of my books, though lately he has been turning them down. I have to be nice to both of them."

"Are you sure you want me to come? Won't I just be *de trop*?" he asks her.

"It would make me less nervous. You'll see. And it will amuse and distract them. They will like you. It will be fun," she says, smiling at him in the mirror.

"But won't they want to talk about your work?"

"Oh, not at all! Not over dinner. They will want to talk about other things—the wife will fall in love with you. She's much younger than her husband. You have my permission— no, my command—to seduce her," she says with a laugh, raising her eyebrows, adding, "Good for business."

"Do you want me to make up your face for you?" he asks. Sometimes he had done this for his mother, who was very beautiful, with her light café au lait skin, her long neck, and her large dark eyes, which she would turn on him so lovingly. He felt she loved him unconditionally. He was both her son and her confidant, her friend. She would weep over his father's infidelity, and he would comfort her, telling her what she wanted to hear: that his father loved her, would always love her best, that she was the most beautiful.

M. nods her head. He makes her lie down on the wide bed with her head propped up on the big white pillow. He sits beside her with her makeup kit. He plucks her eyebrows and removes a hair from her chin. He thinks of the folktale of the woman who needs a love potion and has to get a whisker from the lion to obtain it. M. is quite a lion, he thinks.

He massages her skin with her anti-wrinkle cream. Then he paints her face carefully, applying makeup, masking the lines around her eyes and mouth, hiding the age spots, what the French call "the marks of the cemetery." He outlines her eyes with kohl, rouging her cheeks, puffing powder on her nose. He helps her up and chooses a long black dress with sequins on the bodice. He does up the zipper at the back, clasps a triple string of pearls around her long neck, spreads her diaphanous scarf decorously around her thin shoulders. He sprays a little perfume on her long neck. "Beautiful. Ravishing," he says.

Saying, "You have made me beautiful," M. kisses him on the lips. He stares back at her. She does, indeed, look beautiful and youthful with her white hair shimmering on her shoulders, the long black sheath of a dress that hugs her slender form, her face so skillfully made up, her arms covered with the fine silk scarf, a diamond bracelet that glints in the light. Almost he desires her.

He dresses up in the black pantsuit that she hands him from her closet. He stands beside her so that she can admire him. "*Trés chic*," she says, smoothing down the lapel of the jacket. She takes his arm, and they walk up the road, linked together and laughing like an old married couple. They go through the revolving doors into the Closerie des Lilas at the top of the Rue d'Assas. He has seen it before, read the exorbitant prices on the menu, and imagined how many hungry Ethiopians the price of one of these dishes would feed. M. tells him famous authors have eaten here. "You can order a *bifteck à la Hemingway*, if you like," she says, laughing.

The couple is waiting for them at the bar. Dawit is introduced to M.'s editor and publisher, Gustave, and his wife, Simone. "My most favorite people," M. says, kissing them on both cheeks and once again. The editor is the head of the old and distinguished French publishing house that has published many of her books, a portly gentleman with a thick red neck, broken capillaries in his cheeks, small, astute, slightly slanting blue-gray eyes, and thick white hair carefully slicked back from his forehead. Dawit thinks he looks like Jean

Gabin, whom he has seen in a French film. He wears a shiny gray double-breasted summer suit and a signature ring on his plump pinkie.

His much younger pretty wife is dark-haired, deep-blue-eyed, and small. She lifts her pale face up to Dawit, her dark eyes sparkling with malice and interest. She wears a large square diamond on her ring finger. She writes, too, M. tells Dawit, though nonfiction.

The headwaiter ushers them to a good table on the terrace near the trellis with its climbing plants. The night is warm, the stars visible, the sky an impossible midnight blue. Dawit feels distanced from the scene. What is he doing here with these people in this strange country? He watches himself from afar, as many of the other diners do. They stare at him, the only African in the restaurant, young and well-dressed in his tailored suit, sitting erect beside these older white people. They are wondering, as he is, what he is doing with these people in this celebrated place, while most of his kind suffer quietly. What would Asfa think?

Gustave leans toward Dawit, speaking slowly, as if he might not understand. "We are pleased to meet you. We have heard such good things."

M. puts her hand on Dawit's arm as though he belonged to her. "He's quite brilliant, you know. Speaks so many languages! Perfect French! Even some Italian! He went to Le Rosey in Switzerland as a boy with all the Arab sheikhs, Egyptian royals, the Rothschilds. Imagine! And he's remarkably diligent and efficient! You can't imagine how much energy he has! Up at dawn. Works for hours! It's quite frightening.

Who would have guessed what a dark gem I found in a café? A brown diamond."

Dawit sees the editor's intelligent gaze travel admiringly from his face to his narrow waist and hips. Simone, too, eyes him hungrily from under thick black lashes. They clearly think Dawit is using all this energy for one purpose, and M. seems to enjoy their misapprehension. He smiles at them, batting his long eyelashes and showing off his white teeth in a wide grin, playing the role of the black lover. Like everyone else these French intellectuals are all *au fond* racists, he decides, though they have the good grace to pretend not to be. They are probably considering the length of his penis.

He recalls the many times M. comes to him in the night, waking him from his sound sleep. She switches on the lamp on the piano and asks him to sit on the piano stool and watch, as she does it to herself with her hand. In her pleasure she calls out a name he does not quite catch: perhaps the name of the lover from long ago. She tells him she has never forgotten him, her first and lost love. "He was so much in love with me—but my family ruined it all. My mother made him take us all out to dinner and pay for the entire family, and my brothers were so rude to him—humiliated him." This lover has, probably, been utterly transformed over the years; perhaps he never existed at all.

Now she makes him tell his family stories over the lobster salad, *the gigot d'agneau*, the *flageolets*, and the bottles of pink champagne. Apparently the editor still feels M. is worth treating lavishly, or perhaps it is just an old habit. Dawit wonders if they really like one another. Certainly they seem to enjoy one another's company, the splendid evening, the excellent food. The conversation is lively, filled with allusions to literary life that are difficult to follow. Dawit enjoys the delicate dishes, the champagne, the quick repartee.

Then Simone turns toward him. "Do tell us more about your life in Ethiopia, what it was like there," she urges.

He explains that he was only a child there and often away all year at boarding school in Rolle or in the winter in Gstaad, where the school moved in the winter months. He tells them his father was absent much of the time, following the Emperor to his palaces in Addis Ababa or in Dire Dawa, and increasingly abroad. The Emperor voyaged a lot, particularly in the last years, because he felt more comfortable on these state visits than at home. Everyone wanted to go along, but Dawit's mother would often remain behind in Harar, where she was busy with good works, the schools, the hospital, the Ras Makonnen, which was near the palace. She was often with the Orthodox clergy, who huddled around her. Mostly, in boarding school, he was terribly homesick, he confesses. They treated him with a certain deference because his nobility was stressed, but to them he remained an African boy. He learned to ski, to play tennis, to ride horseback, and to play poker. He spent his time reading books. He says he knows very little about the Emperor's complicated politics, though he would overhear things his father said.

"What was the Emperor like?" Simone wants to know, turning toward him with interest.

His experience with the Emperor was that of the beloved child of a close and trusted associate. He still remembers waking one night as a little boy in his crib and finding the

Emperor leaning over him, giving him his blessing. When Dawit was a child, the Emperor seemed extraordinary, with his small body and big head. He spoke many languages, remembered everyone's name and what they did and had done. He could be extremely charming. Dawit remembers the sparkle in his eyes.

M. urges him to tell them about the pillows. "It's a wonderful story. It reminds me of the one Nabokov told me about the matches. The ones which an admiral used to show Nabokov the sea when he was a little boy," she explains, using her fine hands to show the flat, calm sea and then forming her long fingers into a steeple to show how the admiral placed the matches to show a rough sea. "And then later, when he and his father were running away during the Russian Revolution, they met an old homeless man with a sack around his shoulders, walking across a bridge in St. Petersburg, I think it was. The man asked Nabokov's father for a match to light his cigarette, and in the flare of the match he saw it was the admiral from long ago." She knows everyone, has even known Nabokov.

He tells his pillow story, and everyone looks at him with great interest. "What wonderful details," Simone says, clapping her small hands. "The dangling feet. I knew that Haile Selassie was a small man, but I never realized they would place him up high like that."

"So that he would appear to be above everyone else," Dawit says, looking down at her.

Seeing them all turn toward him and watch him in silence with great interest, he is obliged to go on. He feels as he did as a boy at the dinner table, when the grown-ups turned toward him with interest and tenderness, encouraging him to speak.

Of course, later, toward the end, it was not clear to him if the Emperor was really aware of the severity of the drought and the terrible famine it caused, he tells them. At that point, in 1974, he was very old and probably senile. Most of the people in his circle were preoccupied, it seemed to Dawit, by protocol and their own status, rather than telling the Emperor what he needed to know for his own and the country's sake. Dawit tells them he heard stories of people giving themselves up to the Derg, offended that their names had not been called with the other famous ones!

As with the French Revolution, a bad harvest, famine, and rising prices exacerbated what was already a dire situation. Then the military revolted, just as it had long before in 1928 when Haile Selassie came into power. It took control of radio and television, and spread information about vast sums of the Emperor's money hidden in Switzerland while the people starved.

Simone questions him about his own life there. He feels her move her knee toward his, and he gently presses his leg against hers, smiling with complicity at M. He feels obliged to speak, though he hesitates to tell his terrible tale.

He says he remembers the sudden silence in the streets and looking out the window at the heavily armed troops, the army jeeps everywhere. The atmosphere in the palace was probably much like that in the French court during the Revolution. People had come from all over the country looking for security around the Emperor, still believing he could protect them, despite his age-altered mind, his inability to rule.

They slept all over the palace, huddled together in stunned disbelief, as the courtiers fled the sinking ship, going abroad, deserting, trying desperately to save their own skins. Only a few remained loyal in the end. His mother—he says her name, Sarah—was one of them.

He speaks of her dancing on the edge of the precipice, unable to imagine what was up ahead. He tells them the tale he was told by one of the ministers detained with his father who, unlike his father, survived: how the two of them were called during a luncheon to go to Menelik Palace, which was now the office of the Derg. There, about two hundred men were imprisoned in two basement rooms, the whole area ventilated only by the gap above a steel door and lit by a fluorescent bulb that burned night and day. They were held for months, beaten and insulted daily, paraded in public. On the night of the twenty-third of November, the door was opened, and the two prefects, chosen by the men themselves, were given lists of names, which they read aloud. They were told they were to be released, but there was no necessity for them to dress. Many of them were in their pajamas. They were handcuffed and pushed into prison vans, and taken to the Akaki Prison. Up until the last moment they believed that the soldiers would abide by their word of honor that they would receive a fair trial. But they were taken out in batches, the Emperor's grandson among them, and machine-gunned to the screams of the common prisoners in the jail, who heard the guns firing and the screams and feared they, too, would be executed. They were all gunned down at night under floodlights.

As he speaks he sees his urbane father with his neat mustache, deep-set dark eyes, upright dignified stance, and author-itative stare caught in the glare of the bright lights, in a line of distinguished men who had served their country. "They killed an elite group of educated men who had led the country, cho-sen simply because of being well-known," he says, clenching his fists on the starched tablecloth. "They were innocent peo-ple, journalists, lawyers, doctors. Of course, there were abuses; there had always been abuses. The Emperor was almost eighty; he could no longer govern, really, but he clung to the fantasy that he was doing so. He was too old! But these men, my father among them, were the ones with the knowhow, the educa-tion, and experience to lead the country. They were killed without a trial. It was a terrible crime. My mother and I heard about it over the radio early the next morning—a list of names read aloud, followed by the statement that they had been ex-ecuted by firing squad and already buried. There was no pos-sibility of claiming the body."

The three of them stare at him with wide eyes, over the remains of the *mousse au chocolat*, the *petits fours*, the cham-pagne. For one giddy moment he is the center of attention again like a child blowing out the candles on a birthday cake. He shuts his eyes. They all murmur, "*Quelle horreur!*" and Simone takes his hand with sympathy and asks what hap-pened to his mother and himself after that. He tells them that a few months later, they, too, were picked up and put in prison, where his mother died of untended wounds. He feels himself tremble as he says the words, suddenly in a rage with everyone, including these white people who are listening with their mouths slightly open. He looks at them with smoldering rage, as though they were the ones responsible for all this carnage. He realizes he has said too much, with too much vehemence; he has shown them what he feels, and he hates them for their indiscreet, probing questions, their idle curiosity. He feels empty, as though he has lost something precious, his pride.

They feel his shift of mood, and there is an awkward silence at the table, with the remains of this splendid dinner incongruously still before them. They look at one another, uncertain of what to say. M. clears her throat and says it is all too terrible, really, to even contemplate: they must change the subject, she cannot bear it. They must speak of other things. "Life must go on," she says to him, then smiles and finishes her glass of champagne.

He has revealed more than he wanted to, more than they wanted to hear, caught up in the bright light of their interest and what he took for sympathy. He has felt obliged to entertain them, and now he has spoken of these deaths, which mean more than anything else in his life. He has spoken in order to sing for his supper. Now they turn from him, from the emptied shell. They talk among themselves about something entirely unconnected to his tragic tale. "Have you heard about Michel's review?" Simone says. "*C'est pas vrai!*" they say, obviously thrilled by someone else's unhappiness. They speak of someone else they all know and he doesn't, and he and his tale of blood and murder are fast forgotten. He has made a fool of himself, speaking of something intimate that they could never really share. He feels deflated, humiliated, pricked and airless like a balloon. He and his most intimate feelings, the tragedy of his young life, his country, are but a moment of diversion.

But when they part, Simone reaches up on the toes of her elegant black shoes to whisper into his ear, "Do come and see me sometime soon, darling. I am quite smitten."

X

"YOU TAKE THE CALLS THIS AFTERNOON, DARLING, I WANT TO work," M. says, waving a bejeweled white hand at him as he sits at her desk in the silk-covered Queen Anne chair. She drifts toward her bedroom. "Say I'm busy or whatever you like. If my editor calls, thank him for the dinner. We should have called him."

Gustave does indeed call. "M.? How are you?" he says, taking Dawit's "Allo" for M.'s, as most people do.

"Fine," Dawit answers in her hoarse man's voice, leaning back into the chair and waving a hand, though there is no one to see it. Increasingly, as he writes or talks in her voice, he feels he is M. He has stepped into her shoes both figuratively and literally.

"Wonderful dinner, thank you so much. Meant to call but was distracted by my book."

"The book? How's it going?" the editor asks, without great interest, it seems to Dawit.

"Sentence by sentence," he says, as she would. He is Dawit but he is also M., talking about her work. Indeed, he is correcting her sentences, improving them. Her work is not what it used to be, he feels. She has lost some of her earlier energy, and he understands why Gustave would have turned it down.

"I have an author in town. He'd love to meet you. Le Clezio. Do you know his work?"

"Of course," he says. He would like to meet the handsome, gifted Le Clezio. He picks up one of the fat pens on the desk and twirls it in his fingers idly, staring at the trees.

"Are you free for lunch next week?"

"May I bring my Dawit?" he says.

"Of course you may, he's fascinating! What a handsome young man: those big black eyes; those slim hips! You lucky thing, you!" he says, chuckling conspiratorially. "And surprisingly smart—so much smarter than the one you had before."

"Indeed!" Dawit says.

Gustave adds, "And by the way, I think my Simone rather fell in love with your Dawit. She can't stop talking about him. You wouldn't want to lend him out would you, just for a night? I was thinking of a birthday present for her at her party. She's turning forty next month, and I'm planning something special. You have to come, if you're still in town. You could deposit the present. I think Dawit would be a gift she might appreciate, don't you? As you said, a brown diamond!" and he guffaws.

Dawit says, "I'm not lending my brown diamond, not even to my most favorite couple in the world." As he puts the pen down on the desk, he clenches his fists.

"All right, all right," Gustave says, laughing. "How about Wednesday at one at the Interalliée with Le Clezio for lunch?"

"Perfect," Dawit says and writes the appointment down in M.'s leather Hermès appointment book in her neat hand. He looks out across the trees at the Panthéon, thinking of the famous dead French citizens buried there.

XI

ONE AFTERNOON, SHE COMES INTO HIS ROOM AND STANDS IN the doorway, leaning against the jamb and listening to him play the piano. Outside it is raining, and the sound of the rain mingles with his music. Sometimes, he plays for hours. He has bought some sheet music and practices more difficult pieces. He finds it is such a pleasure. "You play so well," she says.

She is wearing a loose white blouse, a dark cardigan, and her blue jeans and flat shoes. Most of the time she dresses simply like this, eats little, and leads a Spartan existence. She says, "Sing something for me. I want to hear your voice." She expects him to be able to sing as well, but he cannot. "You can't?" she says, mocking him as well as herself, and he laughs. "I can dance," he says and gets up from the piano stool, taking her hand. He leads her into the big bathroom with the mirror and stands before it, stretches out his arms, and shakes his shoulders. He sees her watching him. "Take off your cardigan," he says, and she obeys.

He teaches her the *esketa*, the traditional Ethiopian dance, as his mother once taught him. While the Parisian rain beats against the bathroom windows, he remembers his last glimpse of her before she was taken away.

It was three years ago, in the summer of '75, before the Emperor's death. He can still see the scene: a rainy day with fog in the air. He had not yet turned seventeen. The officers from the Fourth Division entered the large white and gold room, with its ornate furniture, the gold-edged mirrors. His mother was dancing in a small circle of people who were doing their calisthenics, stretching their arms and legs, jumping around as recommended by the Swedish physicians whom the Emperor had summoned, and who had stayed on despite all of the chaos.

Dawit was standing against the wall, half hidden by a potted palm. He watched closely as the guards of the Fourth Division entered the room and stood and stared around in disbelief. Most of them were so young they hardly had any facial hair, but the lead guard bore a well-trimmed mustache, like Dawit's own father's, which arched above his fat lips. He ordered everyone to stop. "People whose days are numbered, doing calisthenics," he said scornfully, while the others snickered. Dawit's mother just went on dancing, her arms spread, her gaze lifted to the ceiling, her bright fuchsia skirt, woven with gold threads, billowing around her as she turned, while the others, following her lead, continued to jump up and down.

She could not conceive of her country without its Emperor. He was the guarantor of freedom and justice, and also of order and discipline. Whenever she heard of children in trouble, she would say, "They should be sent to boarding school!" He remembers her saying, "Nothing is worse than chaos." Tradition and hierarchy were essential to her.

With a studied, nonchalant air the guard lifted the butt of

his gun and leveled it directly at his mother's chest. Dawit could see it happen and yet he could not move, transfixed. It seemed to him as if someone had lifted her legs from under her and then pushed her backward. She seemed to float, as if in water, and similarly inconsequential. They scooped her up off the floor and took her away to join the other members of the royal family in prison, where, untended, she would die of her wounds. He never saw her again. Soon it would be his turn.

He had managed to escape with one of the ministers and some of his mother's jewelry that had been hidden in the garden, before he, too, was picked up, soldiers coming to the house and finding flyers for a student organization that he had promised to distribute. He was accused of being part of the SFD, Students for Democracy, and thrown into prison. He was only seventeen at the time.

Now Dawit stands in front of the mirror and has M. copy his gestures, but he is remembering his mother absurdly dancing to her death while M. learns to shake her bony shoulders like a white butterfly.

PART TWO

❖

The Bay of Foxes

XII

THEY ARRIVE AT THE VILLA ABOVE CALA DI VOLPE AT THE beginning of July. In the early evening light they park the car on a steep incline in the garden under a straw awning and walk down the stone steps to the front door. Blue plumbago, pink hibiscus, and orange *amanti del sole* grow along the path. In the distance Dawit sees the sweep of the vast, tranquil bay with the sparkling blue sea lit up with the sun's dying rays. The scent of the mysterious herb M. has spoken of is in the air, the scent that will always mean Sardinia to him.

She opens the front door, and across the entrance hall he sees the grand living room, a wide terrace, and the scintillant sea. After the tiring drive along narrow streets and winding roads, listening to M. tell him not to drive so fast, grinding her teeth as he took the curves, he is suddenly filled with a surge of joy and gratitude. He sweeps her up in his arms to carry her inside this beautiful home. "My bride," he says extravagantly, laughing. Her body feels heavy, as she drops her head back over his arm, her long hair hanging down. She throws out her arm in a dramatic gesture. He has still not gained back all his strength, and he staggers a little, panting and laying her down on the white linen couch with its bright hand-embroidered orange cushions.

There is a shiny black grand piano in one corner, angled so that the player can see the spectacular view of the sea. He gets up and plays Debussy's "La Mer" for her, as she lies there on the sofa looking across the sea.

"I'm so happy you are here with me," she says. She adds, "Come, you must see your room. I hope you like it," and rises. She takes him down the whitewashed corridor with its arched ceiling to a room on one side of the L-shaped house. From the window there he can still see the sea and part of the steep garden with its olive trees, vines, and bright hibiscus bushes. His canopied iron bed is painted red. The white-and-red-striped flounces that hang from it, as well as the curtains, were all chosen by M.'s French decorator, who decorated the whole house, she tells him. "She did a good job," Dawit says. "What a beautiful room."

"Come and see mine," M. says. She leads him by the hand to the master suite. In the middle of its large bedroom is a wide bed, with a blue bedspread, hand-embroidered in bright colors, and a blue iron bed-head that spreads like a peacock's tail. A polished wooden desk runs all the way beneath the wide window, which looks over the sparkling bay. The bathroom has a tub the size of a small pool, tiled in gray, that takes, she says, hours to fill.

He thanks her profusely for bringing him to this beautiful place as they sit out on the wide terrace in the warm, soft breeze. He brings her vodka and tonic with the olives he has found in a jar on the kitchen table with a note saying, *"Benvenuto."*

She says the olives are a gift from the couple who take care of the house for her, Michelino and Adrianna. He will meet them.

She is too good to him, he says, sitting on the footstool at her feet, feeling the warm air, and listening to the quiet of the evening. How still it is here, how calm. What a relief to have left the gray and rain of Paris and to find himself again in a warm, bright landscape, surrounded by the familiar vegetation of his youth. It is M. who has given him this opportunity to escape to the sun. She gives him a generous monthly allowance and, above all, the security he needs. She has somehow obtained a passport with a temporary travel visa for Italy for him. And now she has brought him to this place.

She tells him a little about its history, how the Aga Khan had seen the island from his yacht and fallen in love with the clear water, the wild, unspoiled land. He had bought up the territory in the area from the local farmers and developed it, keeping it as pristine as possible, preserving much of the local vegetation, ensuring that the houses were low and inconspicuous, nestled into the side of the coast, not allowing any high-rises or garish neon signs. There are wonderful small beaches. The perfectly clear green water earned it the title of Costa Smeralda, the Emerald Coast.

Early the next morning, he runs down the hill past the smooth green golf course of the Pevero, designed, M. has told him, by a famous American, Trent Jones. He comes to the small beach, the Piccolo Pevero, on the other side of the hill. In the silence and the bright light he runs across the beach and up a gentle slope, a sheltered, sunny area with low shrubs and grapevines. The wild flapping wings of a bird break the stillness. He stops for a moment, falls to his knees in the warm white sand. He looks up at the smooth sky, the sea through the bushes, clasps his hands together, and says a prayer of thanksgiving, overcome with gratitude at the bounty of the Lord. Then he goes on over another hill and down onto a small beach, where he plunges into the cool, clear waters of the Mediterranean. He swims out and turns on his back to survey the beach. A gull swoops down low, hunting for its prey, its shadow on the water. In all this dreamy landscape, everything, including his own dark body in the water, contributes to what seems perfection.

"I am so lucky to be here with you," he tells M., when he brings her breakfast in bed on a tray later in the day, a red hibiscus peeping out of the folded white napkin. "I'm so grateful to you," he says, sitting on the bed beside her, taking her hand. He is grateful and tries here, too, to make himself useful.

He continues to listen to her read from her new book. In the evenings before dinner they sit outside on the terrace in the wicker chairs with their feet up on footstools covered in white canvas. She sits in her loose silk trousers and high-necked blouse, drinks vodka, and reads slowly. Her hoarse man's voice rises and falls monotonously. He listens carefully and murmurs his approval, though often now he finds her writing repetitious, exaggerated, and finally dull. It is too much her private fantasy. The word that comes to him is *self-indulgent*, though he does not say that aloud, too afraid of offending. He is so delighted to be here, and too afraid of banishment. But, despite his efforts to listen, he is continuously distracted by thoughts of his dead parents, his compatriots dying of famine, the war-torn country he has left behind, and the poverty of his friends in Paris, the waste of so many worthy lives, to be moved by her depictions of unfulfilled desire.

How easily our heads are turned by fame, is what he thinks, and how dangerous fame is, distancing the writer from the world around him or her. He watches her sip her drink in her elegant gray and black clothes. Then she resumes her reading, waving a bejeweled hand in the air. How can she believe that this is worth writing about? How can she not be aware that someone might find this private fantasy tiresome? She writes about an older woman like herself, with her long white hair, slim body, and desire for a beautiful young black man, who closely resembles himself. There is a lot about long limbs, glowing ebony skin, and large, luminous black eyes. She writes from both the man's and the woman's point of view, switching back and forth between the two characters and back and forth in time confusingly, though she writes all in the present tense with very little about the characters' pasts. Everything happens in the moment, and both of them sound the same to him. There is little dialogue. Nothing much happens between them. The woman desires the man, but he does not desire her. The place with the sea, the heat, a sleek white boat that skips over the clear water is described at length. Dawit says polite things about the hypnotic flow of the sentences and the incantatory cadences of the words, but what he means is that it puts him to sleep— indeed, he finds that he is nodding off and quickly shakes his head.

Every night she leaves him what she has written that day, saying, "Have a look at it again in the morning, will you, darling? I don't want to make a fool of myself." Of course, he says, and shortens the sentences, moves the story along, takes out the chaff, though he still feels the text has no real life in it.

He polishes his Italian, too, diligently with the help of

an Italian grammar book in the early afternoons, lying out on the terrace under the awning. He enjoys the sound of the words, which he says aloud.

He takes pains to make friends with the Sardinian couple who work in the house, the couple who left the olives for them. He thinks of his mother telling him as a boy always to be polite to the servants, all of them, even the dark-skinned Oromo. "In the end they are the most important people, you will find out," his mother would warn prophetically. While M. sleeps, he often takes his breakfast sitting in the kitchen with the couple, who come, they tell him, from the village nearby, Abbiadori, where they live in a compound with their extended families.

Adrianna is a young and pretty woman with large dark eyes and a mole on the side of her cheek. She smokes surreptitiously in the kitchen, when M. is absent or asleep. Though M. smokes herself, she does not like her maid to do so, and complains that the house smells of smoke. Michelino, as his name indicates, is diminutive, a small man, and, Dawit can see, fiercely loyal and honest. M. is an exacting employer, but they voice no complaint. They are both hard workers, and he likes both of them sincerely. "You are my professors. You are teaching me Italian," he says and slips them a few bills surreptitiously.

"*Non! Non! Troppo, signore!*" they say, politely protesting.

They talk to him at length over the breakfast table, sipping cups of delicious coffee and sharing the big sticky buns they bring from their own house, infinitely patient with his stumbling Italian, which improves fast. They tell him about their dreams for a better life for their little girl, Rosetta, a plump, sulky, sallow-skinned child whom Dawit meets when he accepts an invitation to dinner. Secretly, he is afraid the child will be hopelessly spoiled and, if she is not gifted, which she doesn't appear to be, will be unable to take advantage of this wealth of doting interest.

He talks to Michelino while he works, busy with the maintenance around the house, unblocking a drain that is stopped up, cleaning out gutters. He works on a stone wall on the edge of the property, carrying heavy stones and piling them up and securing them with cement that he brings to the villa in large bags. Though M. employs two men who work in the hillside garden, Dawit sometimes works beside them in the bright sunlight, at peace in the warmth and silence of the place, in his light clothes, shorts, his chest bare, digging, weeding, or planting flowers, his hands in the earth. The sort of plants that flourish here are not unlike those in the garden of the mansion in Harar: pink and yellow hibiscus, olive trees, cypresses, *amanti del sole*, dahlias, bright purple bougainvilleas that climb up the patio wall.

M. laughs at him, because she says everything reminds him of Ethiopia. It is particularly true in Sardinia, which seems to him closer to home, with its bright light, endless summer sunshine, and blue skies, the brilliant flora, and the wind, which blows so frequently here: the sirocco, bringing sand from the African desert, or so people say. Sometimes, standing in the garden, he opens his mouth when the wind blows, and imagines the sand from his homeland entering inside him. He misses his mother, his father, Solo, and his friends in Paris, the sound of his own language. Even the Dante he tries to read in the afternoons to improve his Italian speaks to him of his life in Ethiopia, heaven suddenly appearing as Dante exits from hell, those brief moments of reprieve in a violent life.

Laughingly he plays the chauffeur for M., driving her car, parking the white Jaguar under the straw awning, on the steep incline, opening the door for her with a mock bow. Sometimes, as the summer advances and the crowds grow, she finds the beach at Cala di Volpe or the Piccolo Pevero too crowded. She wants to be alone with him. "Let's take a picnic tomorrow and go to the islands. You can drive the boat for me."

She has the couple prepare a picnic basket, and they drive down to the harbor at the hotel of Cala di Volpe and leave the car in the parking lot under the eucalyptus trees. He helps her into the long white motorboat, which she keeps tied up there. He starts the outboard with one quick, strong pull, and the motor turns over, churning water. He sits at the back of the boat and steers it out of the harbor and across the smooth, clear sea. He enjoys the sensation of speed, of the powerful boat skimming fast across the water. She reclines on the white cushions in the prow of the boat, in her large floppy cream hat, her gauzy white cover-up, staring at him. "You are my Virgil," she says, laughing at him. "Lead me where you will," but she tells him where she wants to go.

He takes her out to the islands for their picnic. She points out Mortorio, which she says is one of her favorites. "There! Over there!" she says, which is where they go. He throws the anchor over the side in shallow water at a short distance from the pink sand. He hops out, lifts her up, and carries her, laughing, to shore. He balances the straw picnic basket on his head and then the cushions. He spreads the cushions out on the sand under the big white umbrella, which he drives deep into the sand so the wind will not carry it away. They have the whole beach to themselves: the long grasses, the rocks, and the clear sea. "It has looked like this since the beginning of time," M. says, when he points out a rock perched precariously on top of another. He spreads out the food on a checked tablecloth on the sand. Adrianna has packed prosciutto, figs, cheese, and the flat bread that is called *carta da musica*, music paper, that he loves. They drink red wine from red plastic beakers.

She reclines in the shade, her head propped on her hand. She says this is a perfect place, where she would like to be buried, or rather that she would like her body to be left here among the reeds and rocks floating like Ophelia. She is claustrophobic and hates the idea of lying rotting in a closed tomb. "Did you know that Germaine de Staël's mother, Madame Necker, who was married to the finance minister, had herself pickled and placed in a tomb with her husband and eventually Germaine—because she was so afraid of being buried alive?" He shakes his head in wonder and tells her of the small, airless spaces he has had to endure, that seemed like a series of coffins. In the security of this sun, pink sand, and the clear sea that stretches for as far as the eye can see, he tells her his story.

He recounts the tale of his ghastly voyage to freedom, first to the coast, hidden in the back of a truck, the hills disappearing and the flat land spreading around him as he peeped out at it from time to time from under a blue tarpaulin. He remembers the sun overhead, the sand in his mouth, the scorching heat, the children who waved to him when he stuck his head up for air, the villages with their once-thatched huts so often razed to the ground.

Then there was the dreadful sea voyage to France from Djibouti. With the small amount of money he had got from the sale of his mother's jewelry, he had bribed an official to smuggle him on board without papers or a ticket. He lay in the hold, buried in a box in the dark for days on end, sick and sore and already terribly homesick. The faces of his family: his mother's dark curls, the scar on his father's cheek from a childhood accident, the smell of their skin, the feel of their hands, the sounds of their voices, all of this was already going from him. They, who had come to him under torture, sustaining him, keeping him alive, were now fading, as the ship drew farther and farther away from his homeland. His stomach heaved with the dreadful rising and falling of the ship, his heart contracted in that dark, airless space, with the fear of discovery, his rapidly diminishing supply of food and water, the endless days of renewed and excruciatingly cramped captivity.

"You have suffered so terribly. And are you happy now, darling?" M. asks him, taking his hand and looking into his eyes with longing.

"Very happy. Are you?" he asks.

"Terrifyingly happy," she says.

XIII

He enjoys her company, their idle days together, the sun and sea, the warm breezes, the quiet of the place, the delicious meals. She is witty, playful, and tender with him. She has the ability to laugh at herself. Sometimes she reminds him of his father, who had such a gift with words, and he remembers the dinners in the mansion with the lively and intelligent conversation, the puns and clever repartee. Also, she knows everyone, as his father did in his society of the time, and like many writers she is happy to pass on the intimate details of other famous lives. He could listen to her gossip for hours. She knows about Louis XVI's sex life and how Nabokov's wife carried his books for him when he taught at Cornell. She has read so much and has flashes of real brilliance and insight into the human mind, though there are subjects she ignores completely. She is terrible with figures and seems to have only a very vague acquaintance with geography. Her spelling is atrocious. Above all, her generosity never ceases to surprise and move him. He loves her for being so loving to him. From the start, he wonders why she is this way, and whether her generosity might ever wane. What would happen to him if she ever tired of him? "I want to try and undo some of the harm we have done to you and your people," she says, staring at him lovingly, and he wonders if such an estimable sentiment is true, and how long such altruism might last.

He knows from reading her work that she can be cruel. He remembers reading about her role in France during the Nazi occupation, when she worked to suppress certain publications that spoke out against Pétain by denying them access to the paper they needed to be printed. He remembers her book on the war where she was more concerned about her lover than her Jewish husband, who was starving in a concentration camp.

There are times now, too, when this cruelty emerges. She likes to dine at the restaurant of the splendid hotel at the foot of the hill, Cala di Volpe. They sit outside on the terrace under the stars in the warm air. The service is excellent, and the food delicious. One evening, though, he watches nervously as the young busboy, a fresh-faced island youth, who is replenishing her glass, accidentally brushes against M. When he leans over to refill the bread basket, she stares at the boy, and Dawit sees her eyes flash with a sudden dislike. She is angry in a way Dawit has never seen before, something smoldering and spiteful. "You keep coming too close to me," she snaps at the boy, who has no idea what this white-haired signora is talking about. "*Scusi, signora,*" he says, flushing bright red, hanging his head, humiliated and terrified, Dawit imagines, of losing his lucrative job at this elegant hotel that is, probably, keeping his entire family alive.

She can be stingingly abrasive with anyone who shows stupidity. At a large cocktail party, at a French family's grand villa overlooking the sea, Dawit watches a blond, red-faced young man come rushing up through the crowd on the terrace in his pink Lacoste shirt and loafers. He pushes his way toward her eagerly, coming up close, his champagne flute in hand, red in the face and obviously thrilled to find this celebrated writer at this event and to accost her and show off his knowledge of her work. Perhaps he is a little drunk. Dawit listens in horror as he praises M. fulsomely, saliva flying in the bright air, but for a popular book she has not written. He has mixed up his names and authors.

She just stares back at him for a dreadful moment of silence while he goes on grinning foolishly, waiting for her response. She says, "That is a book I not only didn't write but would never have wanted to. You have not only no memory, young man, but no taste." Dawit wonders how the young man can leave the party intact, and if he goes home and slits his wrists. Indeed, he seems to crumple before Dawit's eyes as he excuses himself and beats a hasty retreat. Dawit recalls the moment in the restaurant with M.'s editor.

But with him she is invariably perfect, loving and thoughtful. She does not interfere in his life; rather she encourages him to go out at night after dinner. "Go to the bars. You need to be with people your own age, your own kind. Play the field. There is safety in numbers, I feel. I understand, you know, I, too, was young once," she says, smiling at him mischievously.

He laughs, says he's too tired. He's been swimming and running and learning Italian all day. He's going to bed. She insists, says he must feel free to do what he wants, to exercise, too. "I want you to be healthy and happy after so much suffering," she says. "Take the car. Running is fine, but why don't you join the tennis club, too? It's very nice and relatively inexpensive. Play some tennis. It would be good for you. You'll meet other young people there."

He decides he will take a tennis lesson. It is ages since he has played. He learned to play as a boy in Switzerland and plays very well. It is a sport he likes particularly. He makes an early morning appointment at the tennis club in Porto Cervo, where he meets Enrico.

XIV

WITH THE TOP DOWN, HE DRIVES THE JAGUAR INTO TOWN AT dawn. The first light of day barely illumines the sky as he parks the white car outside the club. He finds the young tennis pro waiting for him on the tennis court, its purple morning glories growing up the fence around it.

The pro sends him an easy forehand, and Dawit slams the ball back hard, aiming for the corner and thinking of the guard in the prison who tormented him. The pro responds in kind, returning the ball to the other side of the court, setting up a difficult backhand for Dawit. But Dawit responds with a fierce cross-court, a ball the pro is unable to retrieve. "You have a wicked backhand," the tennis pro says, laughing, coming up to the net to retrieve a ball, smiling at him, panting. He runs back and forth across the court, sweating, all through the game.

Out of the corner of his eye Dawit notices someone standing at the fence, watching their game. There is something mysterious and melancholy about the man's fine face. He seems to have something ancient about him, though he looks relatively young, probably in his early forties, the lines around his eyes only adding to his attractiveness. From the way the man stands, feet apart, idly tilting his curly head back slightly in the sunlight, Dawit comes to the conclusion he is someone of privilege, though there is no indication of any belief in his ability to prevail. On the contrary there is something endearingly tentative about the way he stands there considering them, turning his head back and forth, his lips slightly parted with interest.

He comes onto the court as Dawit is leaving. In the gold light of the early morning, as he picks up a ball, Dawit notices the reddish hairs on his bare, freckled legs. An amber-eyed man with curly reddish hair and a delicate profile, he looks as though he has stepped out of a Renaissance painting despite his Lacoste shorts and V-necked tennis sweater. He has the lesson after Dawit's.

"Would you consider playing with me? You are awfully good," he says in Italian, with a charming smile. "I'm afraid you would beat me hollow with that killer backhand." Dawit smiles at him, says he would be delighted to beat him, and they exchange amused glances. The tennis pro introduces them, and they shake hands across the net. Enrico asks Dawit if he would like to have breakfast with him after his lesson. Would Dawit mind waiting for him? "I have all the time in the world," Dawit says and grins. He feels as if he could wait forever for this man.

He takes a long shower, dresses, and sits at the bar in the small restaurant with its climbing plants, a mirror running along the wall behind the bar. He orders a bottle of mineral water and waits for Enrico, excited at the prospect of this encounter, hoping his Italian is up to an extended conversation, which it turns out to be. Enrico speaks clearly, simply, and slowly enough for Dawit to understand, and above all he uses his hands so expressively, he hardly needs words. They sit side by side on the bar stools and order cappuccinos and sticky brioches, and Dawit watches him move his hands. Enrico tells him he is an architect and painter and lives in Rome. He comes from an ancient Roman family, though they have no money any longer, he says. "We are the poor cousins," he says with a charming, self-deprecating laugh and an elegant gesture, though he still has to spend his Sundays during the year in the Vatican, parading about in black as a papal guard.

"What are you doing here?" Dawit asks.

They are here for the summer. His wife is from a prominent Sardinian family. They are powerful politicians Dawit has heard M. mention. They own many newspapers and television stations on the mainland. The family are rather awful, according to Enrico—*prepotente*, he says, grinning, which Dawit does not understand at first but eventually gathers means they are rather full of themselves—but they have been helpful with his career, Enrico admits. Without them he's not sure what would have happened to him, he says. He has built some of the new houses in the vicinity, thanks to his in-laws, he says with modesty. "They know everyone," he explains with a shrug and an expressive gesture. Their own house, which Enrico designed, too, is in Liscia de Vacca on the beach. There are two young children.

Dawit listens to him talk with pleasure, watching his freckled hands hovering over the meaning of words like spotted butterflies over flowers. They remind him of a conductor using his hands to express the meaning of the music.

"What about you? What brings you here?" Enrico asks, looking at him with curiosity in his light brown eyes.

Dawit finds himself speaking in his halting Italian about his past, his country. "Ah, so you are from the oldest place in the world—Ethiopia, the birth of humanity!" Enrico says, smiling. Dawit speaks frankly as he has not done for a long while, of his recent days in Paris, his inability to find work, his crushing poverty. His lack of fluency enables him to say more than he might have in French or even in his own language. He finds that words without any childhood connotations are somehow easier to use. Or perhaps it is that Enrico seems so frank and open, Dawit is encouraged to be equally so. He says he is staying with a famous writer who has befriended him. She has a villa above Cala di Volpe.

"Who is it?" Enrico asks, and Dawit tells him.

Enrico knows M.'s work. He knows her villa, too. He is visibly impressed and makes an expression of awe, opening his eyes wide and pulling down his lips at the corners. He knows the architect who built the villa, a distinguished older man, Vietti. It was one of the first houses on the hill. "*Una villa bellissima*," he says, looking at Dawit, obviously considering him anew. Then he asks him, "Are you two . . . involved?" crossing two fingers in the air to make his meaning clear.

Dawit shakes his head. "She's an interesting woman and she has been very good to me, but how *could* I be?" he says and looks at Enrico.

"Because of her age?" Enrico asks.

"Not only that," Dawit says, looking into his eyes and then lowering his gaze.

"Oh, I see. *Bene!*" Enrico says with a flash of white teeth, a frank smile which is always a surprise in his melancholy face. "I have to go now, but I hope we can meet again soon. I'd like to get to know you better."

Later Dawit meets an adorable little boy with blond hair and flushed cheeks who is perched on Enrico's shoulders, his hands gripping his father's thick russet curls. Dawit thinks of Takla with a lonely tilt of the heart.

X V

THEY DO NOT COME TO THE VILLA WHEN THEY SPEND AFTER-
noons together. They meet at the tennis club in Porto Cervo.
Dawit feels he cannot see enough of Enrico. He knows he is
moving back to Rome at the end of the summer, that their
time together will be brief. Each moment is precious. When
he is not with Enrico, he replays their time together in his
mind like a film. He finds it difficult to think of anything
else, to concentrate on what M. is saying to him.

"How can you play tennis in the heat of the day?" M. asks
him, looking worried.

He shrugs. "You know the heat doesn't bother me."

"Ah, youth," she says and smiles with fond indulgence.

They do, indeed, play tennis in the heat of the day. Dawit
usually beats Enrico, but sometimes he concedes out of pity.
Then they have a quick shower, a light lunch in the restaurant, a glass of white Sardinian wine. Afterward they use one
of the upstairs rooms.

There, in the small white room, with the shutters drawn,
Enrico's pale skin glows as he lets Dawit undress him. Dawit
loves the freckles on his shoulders and back. With a half smile,
complicitous and yet slightly ironic—there is often something

slightly detached about Enrico—he allows Dawit to enter his body with passion. They make love to the accompaniment of the *pong* of the tennis balls hit back and forth and an occasional expletive in the air.

Enrico loves pleasure. He whispers in a low, almost strangled voice into Dawit's ear. He tells him he loves his smooth black skin. "How you shine for me!" he says, calling him his Dark King, his Balthazar, a wise man come to adore the child. He makes love passionately, using his nails and teeth, his tongue, as though he wishes to absorb more and more of Dawit's body, his strength and youth.

Even so, he is often in a hurry, checking the time, afraid of leaving late and arousing his wife's suspicion. He fears discovery. Obviously, he is a devoted husband, son-in-law, and father. He is the one who tells Dawit when they can meet and for how long, saying succinctly, "I have an hour tomorrow afternoon," without further explanation. Dawit often feels Enrico is halfway out the door, only giving himself up completely for a moment at the height of passion. From the second he enters the room, he is ready to leave, folding his clothes neatly on the chair, leaving his car keys—he drives an old Alfa Romeo—available.

Only if his wife is absent for the afternoon or is at her parents' house with the children does he permit Dawit to tarry on the bed beside him with the shutters drawn and the sound of the tennis players below. As long as Dawit is home by seven in the evening to hear her work, M. does not seem to mind.

Enrico gazes at the ceiling, and Dawit encourages him to

talk about his life. He wants to know everything about him. Also, he loves lying beside him and listening to the sound of his patrician voice, with its Italian cadences, which he doesn't always understand but sound to him like singing. He feels he has entered an Italian opera, one about love and death.

He thinks of his father, who loved Italian opera and particularly *Aida*, with its Ethiopian story, which he listened to again and again.

Dawit lies quietly and stares at Enrico's small, almost pointed ears, his endearingly boyish curls, his fine profile, with the pointed nose, almost pencil-thin at the tip, the sensuous lips. He adores the slight swell of the stomach and the dusting of reddish hair on the pale skin that goes with it. Dawit winds his own dark arm around Enrico's white waist to hold him gently, caress his soft, freckled skin. "Together, we make art," Enrico says.

Dawit watches the way Enrico stands on one foot, leaning slightly against a wall, the tilt of the hip, the tentative, soft-footed, graceful walk. Even his tennis, the steady game he plays, hitting the ball regularly, elegantly, but never with much force, Dawit finds endearing. Somehow, Enrico's delicacy moves Dawit more than a muscular frame would have. He seems vulnerable, boyish, easily swayed. Dawit wants to protect him despite his worldly success as an architect, despite his rich wife, his powerful family, his aristocratic antecedents. He seems unsure of himself in so many ways, always sees both sides to every question, vacillating, uncertain. "You may be right," he often says, laughing, shrugging his narrow shoulders.

He talks about his life in Rome. He is in love with Rome and proud of his city as only a Roman can be. He says, "It's so beautiful. Every time you turn a corner it is with an orgasm. The Romans are so beautiful, too, even the policemen in their white helmets in the summer with their batons lifted are beautiful."

He invites Dawit to visit. He wants to show him the streets, the monuments that he loves particularly: the little circular temple of Vesta in the Roman forum—he makes a gesture to convey his admiration. He offers to find him a job, perhaps even at the firm where he works. Dawit must bone up on his Italian. "With your gift for languages, it would be easy enough. It's amazing how much Italian you've learned in a few weeks. It would be great to have you there," he says. He laughs when Dawit sometimes uses the archaic words he has found in Dante. "You are too much," he says. "You speak archaic Italian! You must come and stay in Rome. We could see one another every day." He tells Dawit he goes every evening to have a drink with his widowed mother before dinner, and she is a wonderful alibi and always understanding

"How lucky you are!" Dawit says, thinking of his own mother and how understanding she was.

Dawit imagines a small apartment in Rome, a job, the possibility of spending every evening with Enrico, above all his own freedom. They even speak of living together openly, but Dawit is quite aware this is just a fantasy, as is most probably the job at the architectural firm in Rome. Enrico's position, if Dawit has understood rightly, though he is a good architect, still depends largely on his wife's family's powerful influence as the source of his commissions. Besides, Dawit is certain this man would never leave his wife or do anything to jeopardize his marriage.

The wife, of course, knows nothing about this secret summer life. Enrico says he feels terrible about her. She is young and lovely and loves him very much. "Lying is a lonely business, *amico mio*," he says remorsefully.

XVI

Sometimes, after making love, they leave the tennis courts and dare to drive together in M.'s Jaguar with the top down along the coast. They park in an isolated clearing overlooking a small, quiet beach. They sit side by side in silence in the car. Nothing stirs, and all they can hear is the soft, sad lapping of the sea, the lonely cry of a seagull, the monotonous chirring of the cicadas. Everything speaks to Dawit of death. He looks at the calm, clear water, the stunted bushes that grow wild along the coast, and the bullrushes almost pink in the twilight. This lovely place will still be here, eternal and indifferent when he and Enrico are no more.

He does not recount the torture, the beatings of the feet held suspended in the air, or the repeated near-drownings in filthy water, or even the interminable loneliness of his cell, but rather the few moments of reprieve during his imprisonment. Sporadically and inexplicably, he would be dragged out, wounded, bleeding, and half mad from solitude, from his cell. He was allowed to clean himself. The guard removed his shackles, ordered him to undress and shower. He was given disinfectant soap to cleanse his wounds and to scrub at the lice in his hair and the other vermin crawling all over his aching body.

Sometimes, he was allowed to walk about for an hour or so, still shackled but in the light and air of the courtyard. There he would stare up at the sky or fall to his knees at the sight of a blade of green grass and offer up his thanks to God. Green grass! He remembers the thrill of it. A few times he found himself in the company of other prisoners, shuffling around half demented with pain and hunger. Once or twice he spoke to someone else for a moment, sitting shackled side by side, fearing always that what was said might be reported. "How long have you been here?" they would ask. He would shrug his shoulders and say he couldn't tell. "Forever," he would say, for so it seemed. Once an older woman with cracked teeth, blind in one eye, had looked at him sadly and said, "So young to be shut away in darkness," and he was moved by her sympathy.

One evening, they brought an old Orthodox priest into his cell, and he was certain then that they were preparing to execute him the next day. The ancient bearded monk, who spoke French, seemed as terrified as he was but allowed him to read his favorite passages from his Bible. Together they sang the familiar hymns.

Occasionally, he would find with his bread an unexpected boon, a small, wrinkled apple, a bunch of radishes, a raw onion, or a tomato, and once a whole, perfect orange, which he devoured with bliss. He never knew what caused these occasional kindnesses, if they came because of some inspection by a Red Cross agency or were simply the result of some guard's humanity, perhaps even the guard who tormented him so. These moments come back to him vividly, sitting in the car in the twilight beside Enrico.

"How did you get out?" Enrico asks.

Dawit turns to him and tells him some of the story. He describes the guard who tormented him, Solo's appearance in his cell, the gift of the file, and the wait behind the door with the chain.

"What happened?" Enrico asks.

"Eventually, at dawn, someone came, and I was waiting for him and able to do what was necessary to save my life," Dawit says. Enrico turns his head to look at him, opens his eyes wide. "You killed him with your bare hands?" he asks, touching Dawit's hand.

Dawit nods his head and makes a gesture to show how he held the chain around the man's neck and throttled him.

Enrico smiles and pretends to shake. He says, "Such a violent black man!"

Dawit shows Enrico the marks of his nails and teeth on his skin and says, "Such a violent white one!"

Outside the prison, Dawit says, the half-dark streets were filled with flares and absurd cries: "Revolutionary motherland or death!" "Long live Marxism!" "Viva proletariat Ethiopia. Viva Mengistu!"

XVII

As the summer draws to a close, Dawit wonders what M. knows. Nights, she comes frequently now into his room and wakes him by turning on the lamp. He is naked in the high heat of the summer, exhausted after his days in the sun, the running, the swimming, the tennis, and above all the lovemaking. Or rather, when M. wakes him, switching on the small lamp on the heavy wooden dresser, he pretends to sleep, trying to ignore her, hoping she will retreat, but he feels her presence, hears her coming closer, bending over him, studying him. He feels her hot, fetid breath on his cheek. Sometimes she even touches him gently, runs her hands over his back and his shoulders and pushes at his body to turn him. He pretends to stir sleepily, turns over obediently, and curls up on his side. Then she stretches out beside him, her hot, bony body suffocatingly against his. She holds on to him, or she even lies across his body, her mouth over his, puts his hands on her sex, begs him to ease her growing desire. "Please," she says. "Please. I will give you more money, anything you wish."

"I don't need more money. I need sleep. You have given me quite enough money," he says crossly, groaning, half asleep, though he has recently had a letter from Asfa, to whom he had written, giving him his Sardinian address. Little Takla is ill. He has asthma, and the doctor says he needs medicine: cortisone. As the family is illegally in Paris, they have no insurance. So when she insists, he allows M. to augment his monthly stipend, and he sends Asfa a large check. As he withdraws from M. into his mind and Enrico's arms, into his past, she grows hungrier for his caresses, his affection.

She insists on taking him shopping to buy him his own clothes, the expensive items in the elegant shops in Porto Cervo or the one at the foot of the hill that is part of the hotel at Cala di Volpe. She sits in a plush armchair, her thin legs crossed in pale stockings, and taps her long fingers impatiently on the arm of the chair. She has him parade before her in the elegant clothes and watches him hungrily. "That looks divine on you. You must have it," she insists despite his protests. "I don't need it," he says. "Yes, yes, you must take it," she insists. She wants to buy him soft Italian shoes, linen shirts in pale blues, mauves, and pinks, Armani ties, scarves, and well-cut linen suits in white, navy, or black. She even wants to buy him a Borsalino hat. He protests. He says, "I don't need more summer clothes. Besides, everything here is ridiculously expensive." He thinks of the hungry people in his homeland and what they could do with all this money she wants to spend on these unnecessary items.

"You look so good. You are more beautiful every day," she says, admiring him as he strides impatiently before her. She gets up to touch his smooth, dark skin. "My beautiful dark David," she murmurs amorously in his ear. He sees the young salesgirl, who stands with yet another linen suit over her arm, watching them with an amused glance that seems to say, *Just take the clothes. You deserve them.*

It is true he has grown more muscular with all the exercise, the lovemaking, and the good Sardinian food. He gluttonously gobbles up all the ripe melons, the plump black figs and prosciutto, the tomatoes with mozzarella and basil, the delicious honey on flat bread, the black olives that Adrianna brings from their farm. M., who eats less and less, likes to watch *him* eat. She insists on serving him in the evenings, carrying out the silver tray with the hors d'oeuvres onto the terrace: the black olives, salted almonds, smoked salmon, grilled calamari, bottles of champagne. She presses presents on him: leather-bound books she orders from France, Montblanc pens, tennis rackets and whites and shoes, little ivory boxes for the gold cuff links she buys him. She watches him come and go. "What time will you be home this evening? Don't be late," she says anxiously.

He knows that she studies the marks of Enrico's passion all over him. Nights, he falls back asleep aware that she is still there, hovering over him, pressed against him, watching him sleep, the light still lit as it was sporadically in the prison. Sometimes he wakes with her mouth on his, suffocating him. "I cannot breathe," he says, turning from her. Her constant attention becomes more and more irksome, the disturbance to his sleep, her demands on his body increasingly hard to bear. It begins to make him think of the torture his body was submitted to in prison, the repeated near-drownings, which were the hardest to withstand.

He finds he dreams repeatedly, waking trembling, grinding his teeth and drenched in sweat. He dreams of the moment in his cell when the guard came in. He sees himself as he threw the chain around his neck and pulled as hard as he could, suddenly filled with a rush of savage strength, which seemed to come from elsewhere, from outside himself. He watches as the guard lifts his hands to pull the chain away, searching desperately to free himself, gasping for breath, his eyes staring and seeming to protrude in the flat face. He listens to the final feeble throttled cry that comes from the man's swollen lips, waking with a dreadful start to find M. moaning his name at his side. "Dawit, please, please," she says. "I need you. Help me, darling heart."

XVIII

THIS MORNING, WHEN HE COMES BACK FROM HIS RUN TO THE beach, he finds M. already awake and out on the terrace, sipping coffee in her white silk robe. "You're up early," he says, surprised. Usually he has the morning hours, at least, to himself and can make his escape to the tennis club undetected.

"I couldn't sleep. Couldn't work," she says, looking up at him accusingly, tears in her pale eyes.

It is a hot, still, late August day, the sky a transparent blue, only the monotonous sound of the cicadas, the smell of bitter herbs in the air.

"Shall I bring you some breakfast?" he asks in a conciliatory tone. She purses her lips but nods her head. She eats with him in silence on the terrace, eating from a tray, nibbling at the thin slices of grilled German black bread with a little butter that she eats every morning for her breakfast, and sipping cappuccino from the blue-and-white terra-cotta cups made in the factory on the island. Dawit slathers his bread with butter and delicious Sardinian honey the couple brings them from their farm in the interior of the island as well as the olive oil and the olives they cure themselves. M. is saying something to him, but he is not listening. He imagines the curve of Enrico's spine, the sweet lift of his buttocks. He can feel his body pressed close. He becomes aware that she is watching him closely while he eats. "You know, you have changed. I don't know you. I feel you're not really listening to me at all. You don't hear me. I don't even hear you play the piano anymore," she says with a little catch in her voice. He just looks out at the horizon shimmering in the heat of the day, wondering if he will see Enrico that afternoon.

She goes on, "You have marks all over your body—do you know? Scratches, bites—signs of someone else's lust."

What can he say? Has she not told him herself to go out and enjoy himself? He looks at her pale, thin face, with its pointed nose. She looks back at him, and now he sees an empty look in her blue-gray eyes, something he has never seen there, as though she has withdrawn from him. He remembers how she looked at the busboy who brushed against her accidentally in the restaurant. She is looking at him without seeing him. "You are making me suffer, and I warn you, I don't like to suffer. Unnecessary suffering is distracting and finally just plain stupid. I can't sleep or work, or even eat when I feel like this."

"The last thing I want to do is to make you suffer," he says sincerely, putting down the slice of bread he holds in his hand.

"Well, act accordingly, make sure I don't, then," she tells him with a flash of rage in her eyes. "Don't jeopardize something so precious." She gets up and walks stiffly, awkwardly across the terrace, through the living room, and up the steps, toward her room. He is moved by her distress, her awkwardness.

He makes an effort to be more discreet. He curtails his

afternoons at the tennis club and takes her out to her favorite island for picnics as before. He plays the piano in the evening and listens to her read from her book. He attempts to listen carefully, but his mind wanders.

One afternoon, Enrico calls him to tell him his wife has returned to Rome with the children, so he has the whole afternoon and evening free. It is an offer Dawit cannot refuse. He knows Enrico will soon join his wife and children in Rome. They have little time left.

They linger on in the dimly lit room above the tennis courts until it is late in the day, making love repeatedly with a desperation that verges on violence. Again and again, Dawit enters Enrico's tender white flesh. He cannot bring himself to rise from the bed, to leave him.

When he finally arrives back at the villa, driving dangerously fast along the coast in the Jaguar, it is almost dark. He has missed the magic sunset hour when M. reads her work to him, and when she starts her drinking. Like many alcoholics she has a precise hour when she allows herself to start drinking seriously, though she will occasionally drink beer with lunch; but the vodka and tonics come out at seven in the evening.

He finds her walking up and down on the terrace in a long Missoni dress, the vivid red, orange, and purple stripes emphasizing her pale skin, the dark circles under her eyes. Even in the dim light, he realizes she has lost more weight and looks almost haggard. She has her vodka and tonic in hand, the ice clinking ominously, as she walks in her elegant Italian sandals, waving her burning cigarette in the air with a shaking hand. He can see she must have already drunk several vodkas, her purple lipstick running in the lines around her thin lips, her hair disheveled on her shoulders. Her eyes smolder. She shouts at him. "Where were you? I was worried! I was frightened! I thought something had happened to you! You could have telephoned! I drove into town to look for you, but I couldn't find you anywhere!" He can imagine her rushing up and down the narrow streets of the small town frantically, distraught, making a spectacle of herself in her long, thin dress.

"I'm so sorry I worried you. I forgot the time," he says, looking at the thin Piaget watch she has given him among so many fine things.

She looks at him, her eyes flashing with spite. "I bet you did. I don't mind you going to bars at all hours to find other men, doing whatever *cochonnerie* you want to do with them. I understand that, but I expect a certain consideration, after all I have done for you, and if you want to continue to lead the life I've made possible for you."

He does not know what to say. He lowers his gaze to the terra-cotta tile at his feet. Indeed, he owes her for everything he wears, everything he eats, for the roof over his head. Without her he would have nothing. He feels like a chastised child, a humbled servant. He remembers her shrill voice shouting at the poor concierge in Paris whom she made weep. He, too, would like to weep like a child. He is her chattel, her slave.

She says, "What is happening to you? Are you falling in love?"

He says nothing, looks at her briefly and then away from the rage in her eyes, out across the hills and into the darkness of the night. How can she expect him to be in love with her?

"About yourself you know nothing, do you? You don't seem to know if you are hot or cold."

"You are right about that," he says, though he could tell her that he feels Enrico's presence has spread all through his body like his own blood, burning in his veins like a secret fire.

XIX

ALL THROUGH THE HOT, STILL LAST DAYS OF AUGUST HE AVOIDS Enrico and does not answer his calls or go to the tennis club. Then, one morning—it is early September but still hot in Sardinia, a dry wind blowing wildly in the scrub—he comes back from his morning run and is taking out a bottle of San Pellegrino from the refrigerator when he finds M. in the kitchen. She is already up and dressed in a dark linen suit with a gray blouse, her hair tied back from her face. Over breakfast, which they eat together inside, she tells him she will be away overnight. She is going to Sassari today, on the other side of the island, on some book business, a speaking engagement. She will stay overnight—there is a decent hotel there—and come back the next morning.

Does she not want him to go with her? he asks, leaning forward across the checked tablecloth to touch her hand. "I could drive you there," he offers. He listens to the sound of the wind outside, the sand blowing against the window. She shakes her head without looking at him. She will drive herself. She seems determined, businesslike. She gazes at him dully. She finishes her breakfast fast, adjusts her cloche hat in the mirror in the hall, and allows him to carry her small brown leather suitcase up the hill to her car. "You have forgotten your book," he says as she is getting in, realizing she has left it on the console in the hall. He runs down the stone steps and then back up again to put her latest book beside her on the seat. He kisses her on the cheek through the open window. "Good luck. I hope it goes well," he says, and she just looks at him. He asks again if she is sure she does not want him to accompany her. She shakes her head. He tells her to drive safely, to be careful and watches her drive off in her Jaguar in her smart navy linen suit, her black leghorn hat. He runs down the steps and waves gaily to her from the stone entranceway to the villa as she drives down the hill toward the bay, but she does not turn her head or wave out the window to him.

He goes inside and stands by the telephone for a moment, hesitating, listening to the wind, thinking of M. and her lonely drive along the windy coast, the dead expression in her eyes. At the same time, like an underground stream running continuously beneath the surface, he is thinking of Enrico. He knows he is leaving Porto Cervo within the week to join his wife and children in Rome, where the older girl is getting ready to start school. It is likely to be their last time together.

His heart drumming with hope, he picks up the phone and calls Enrico at the studio where he works with a group of architects in Porto Cervo. He invites him to come to the villa that afternoon. "Leave your car below at Cala di Volpe, in the parking lot in the shade of the eucalyptus, and walk up the hill," he says. They can spend the whole afternoon and night together in the villa.

He leaves the front door open and watches through the

window as Enrico comes in under the stone archway and enters the villa. It gives him so much pleasure to see his familiar form and face here, to think they can spend the whole afternoon and night together in this beautiful place. He goes to him quickly and takes him tightly in his arms. "God, I'm so happy to see you! I'm so glad you are here," he whispers, though he can hear the couple in the kitchen talking in their Sardinian dialect, gathering up their things. "They are leaving," he says, as he has told them to leave after lunch. He beckons to Enrico to follow him through the living room, where he leaves his sweater and the book he is reading on the sofa.

They slip silently down the whitewashed corridor in the shadows of the afternoon and go into Dawit's room at the end of the corridor with its blood-red iron canopied bed and the white-and-red-striped hangings. They pull down the shutters and throw themselves joyously across the double bed. "Now this is my home," Dawit says, taking Enrico up in his arms.

They are side by side at the moment of no return, when Dawit becomes aware of footsteps coming to a halt outside the door. There is nothing much he can do but finish what they have so impetuously begun and then lie there holding his breath, listening. "There is someone out there," Dawit whispers, shifting onto his back. He watches the handle on the door slowly turn. It is like something out of a nightmare.

"One of the servants?" Enrico whispers, but when Dawit looks at him he can see a glint of fear in his light brown eyes. Together they listen to the footsteps on the stone floor outside his room, retreating. Then there is silence again, with only the afternoon sounds of the wind moaning, the cicadas sawing, and the restless murmur of the sea.

"I doubt it," Dawit says, for he has told the couple to go home after their lunch, to take advantage of M.'s absence and have the afternoon and evening off. They never sleep on the premises. There is no reason for them to disturb his siesta, and they would never try his locked door.

"Damn! And I think I left my sweater and a book on the couch in the living room," Enrico whispers.

"Oh, God," Dawit says, thinking of the dead white cushions on the couch and Enrico's distinctive turquoise sweater and the thriller, an Italian translation of a book by Patricia Highsmith that Enrico is reading—not something Dawit would read. Lately he has been reading Italian poetry.

"But you assured me she was away spending the night in Sassari. How could it have been her?" Enrico says in a frightened voice, sitting up now, his head on one elbow. In the half-light of the shuttered room, Dawit can see the sweat on his brow, his damp russet curls, and his bare freckled shoulders.

XX

HE CAN FEEL THE TENSION THAT EVENING FROM THE MOMENT M. appears on the terrace, though she says nothing about the locked door, Enrico's book on the sofa, the sweater she must have seen. She pleads exhaustion, which she maintains has brought about her early return from Sassari. "I couldn't go through with it. A crowd of people showed up, and I was about to read when I just told them I was feeling ill, got in the car, and came home."

"You should have let me come with you," he says, but he wonders if she ever went there or simply drove for a while and then came home. Was this all a test? She looks at him and says, "I'm exhausted and getting old" and that she needs a bath. Indeed, she does look older and sad in her rumpled linen suit and gray blouse. Without her hat her hair is flat and greasy. He offers to run her bath, but she shakes her head and goes slowly up the stairs into her room.

When she emerges from her bath, she has dressed up, put on her makeup, brushed her hair. She has a red cashmere shawl around her bony shoulders, though the evening is warm and still.

They eat the cold food Adrianna has left for Dawit's dinner: prosciutto, melon, artichoke hearts, cold chicken in aspic and cheese, which he spreads out on the blue-and-white-checked tablecloth on the round stone table in the dining area that gives onto a patio behind where the purple bougainvillea climbs up the rock. M. hardly eats, only drinking several glasses of red wine, which she pours for herself, holding the bottle at the neck, her hand visibly shaking. The silence reminds Dawit of that first dinner they ate together in her apartment on the Rue Guynemer when they had sat side by side awkwardly in silence. He gets up and offers to make coffee.

They are sitting out on the wide terra-cotta terrace, sipping the coffee Dawit has served in her gold-rimmed demitasses, when she speaks. She sits upright in the flowing silk trousers and a high-necked black blouse she had changed into before dinner. Her white hair is tied severely back from her face, which makes her nose seem even more sharp, her eyes more slanting. She stares out across the darkening hills and the glittering silver sea in the distance, puts down her cup, and leans forward for him to light her cigarette. There is a full moon illuminating the night sky, so that only the brightest of stars are visible in the vast expanse above them.

In the bright light of the moon, he can see how her eyes snap at him with malice. She is in a rage, smoldering and spiteful, blowing out smoke into the air. As she leans toward him, looking into his face, he can smell her fetid breath.

He thinks of a *kinae* from his childhood. The Capuchin monk who taught him as a young boy asked him to fathom its meaning. There were always two layers that he would have to find, the bronze and the gold. The gold to this particular *kinae* went something like, "Now that you have decided to deny me my due, there is no point in continuing our relationship. I am not one of those who can forget or forgive."

He thinks of Enrico but knows very well what he would do if Dawit arrived with his suitcase on his doorstep. Enrico is not, he knows, a man of courage or even determination. He doesn't pretend to be. It is partly for this, his timidity, his self-deprecating honesty, that Dawit loves him. His weakness is part of his charm, but it makes him someone Dawit cannot count on in an emergency of this kind.

M. puffs on her cigarette, blows out the smoke, and says, "I had an interesting letter some time ago. I didn't consider it seriously at the time, but I did have the foresight to stall. I told them I'd think it over and I would let them know."

Dawit waits for her to go on.

"It was an offer to teach in America."

"Surely you wouldn't consider such a thing?"

He stares back at her. There is no possibility of his accompanying her there, of course, because he would never be granted a visa. He doesn't have a working visa for France. The tourist visa she has obtained for him is temporary and will soon expire.

But M. goes on smoking her Gitane and speaking, waving her fine fingers, telling him about the position she has been offered. "It's a chair at one of the most prestigious places. I wouldn't have to do much teaching, just one course, with all my summers free, a month at Christmas, and sabbaticals. I wouldn't even have to attend many meetings, they assure me. The means to procure a house would be provided, along with a generous salary, health benefits. A distinguished group of professors would be my colleagues. Basically, I would just be lending the program a famous French name. It seems like a wise move at this point in my career, don't you think? I'm not sure how much longer I can churn out books to support myself. In any case, I've decided to write and accept."

"You would start teaching this fall?" Dawit asks.

"I would only have to start next spring, but I'd leave quite soon to look for a house in the area, settle in. It would be a change." She looks at him and smiles in a grim, ghastly way. "I think we both need a change, don't you?" She purses her lips and looks away from him. There is something of the rat about her, he thinks, looking at her profile in the moonlight, or perhaps it is a ferret.

He remembers his arrival in Marseilles, his fear of the police as he made a secret descent from the ship, and the misery of the train ride to Paris followed by a wash of gray days of rain, the cramped quarters, the smell of rotting drains in the crowded apartment in the *banlieue* where Asfa had so generously received him along with all the jetsam and flotsam of African society, the impossibility of finding any work without papers, without degrees or letters of recommendation. And ultimately roaming the damp gray streets, scorned and humiliated, hungry and terrified.

Without M.'s protection, her money and her fame, it is clear to him, and surely to her, what will happen to him. Sooner or later he will be picked up and sent home, where the same government, unbelievably, still clings to its ill-gotten power, despite famine in the land. He will not be as lucky a second time around. His Solomon, alas, is most probably dead, killed in one of the frequent purges.

"You would shut up the apartment in Paris?" he asks, his voice trembling.

"From now on, the apartment in Paris, this villa, as well as the chalet in Gstaad would certainly be shut to you," she says and stubs out her half-smoked cigarette in the large glass ashtray at her elbow. She stares at him without seeing him, her blue-gray eyes blank. He can only stare back, but what he sees is himself, shuffling eight steps to the overflowing plastic bucket in the corner of his cell, the smell of feces and fear in the air, the sensation of his chest pressing into his spine.

Surely M. must know that by banishing him she is sending him back to certain death. Obviously, she no longer cares. She has toyed with him for a while—he has served a certain function—but now she has had enough.

"In fact, I'd like you to be gone by tomorrow morning. Leave your keys on the console in the hall, along with your checkbook, will you? I'll give you something to tide you over, of course, enough to get you off the island, but you'll have to fend for yourself after that. I'll be closing your account in the morning."

He thinks of her telling him how he had brought her youth back into her life. How can he go back to his other life now, after the one he has led with M.? His position has not changed. He has not acquired any degrees, or letters of recommendation, or permanent papers, and no money at all. Foolishly, he has spent all she has given him, giving most of it away, living through her, believing, hoping she would protect him as the courtiers in his homeland had expected the Emperor to do. He has learned nothing from his parents' bitter experience. He has lived a fantasy, playing games, making believe. She well knows he has nothing to sustain him.

"What will I do?" he asks, his voice shaking, folding his fingers to stop their trembling. How can she abandon him so easily? Does she want him to go back to his country, back to prison? Is she trying to kill him? When he looks into her eyes, he feels, indeed, that her rage is such that she would like him dead.

"You're an enterprising young man. You've survived so far. In fact, you've been very lucky. We've had a good summer together, haven't we? We have brought each other a moment of reprieve." For a moment she seems to see him again, and her eyes fill with tears. Will she relent, change her mind? But she quickly regains control of herself and goes on, "Let's leave it at that. I'm sure you'll figure it all out. Perhaps you could do some sort of secretarial work for someone else? I'm sure someone will pick you up, as I did, take pity on you. You tell your story rather well, I must say. A few tears and you'll be in someone's arms. You are so young, heartbreakingly beautiful, and very smart, to boot—an excellent secretary," she says, then waves her hands in the air and looks at him now as though he were some sort of merchandise she was considering but has now decided is entirely unnecessary.

She rises stiffly and strides across the stone floor into the living room, where he follows her. He considers going down on his knees, weeping, as he did that first day in the café, or jumping up on the brick wall, threatening to throw himself off the cliff, but he senses it would not change her decision. She would just allow him to jump. In her furor she is like a rock, unbreakable, immovable. Besides, his pride prevents him from begging. He can only watch her go. He can see that her excessive passion has changed into excessive hate. She is bent on humiliating him completely.

She bends over and opens up her safe, which is in an alcove in the wall beside the sofa. She pulls out a small stack of bills, puts them on the inlaid table beside her, closes the safe, and twists the knob. "This will get you off the island. I expect you to be gone by noon tomorrow. I don't like lingering good-byes. You can take the Land Rover and leave it at the airport. Put the keys under the mat. I'll have Michelino come and pick it up. You'd better start packing tonight. Take whatever clothes you want. At least you'll be well dressed this time. I'm going to take some sleeping pills and try and get some sleep." And she walks away and goes up the steps to her bedroom without a backward glance, or another word.

XXI

He walks back and forth in his room in the heat and silence of the quiet summer night. Then he stands at the open window for a while. He looks out at the scintillant sea in the moonlight. His whole life rushes back to him like a wave, as though he were drowning in his humiliation—as his torturers once almost drowned him or as if he were about to face his own execution. Indeed, he feels death is close. What happens now will determine his future and somehow even his past, all that had gone before since his and his mother's and father's births. This moment had always awaited him.

Memories from his childhood come to him: the dawns in Harar, with the smells of overripe fruit and wood smoke in the air, the cries of the hyenas disappearing at dawn, the crescendo of birdsong in the lime and pomegranate trees, the calls to prayer from the ninety-nine mosques, the bells from the church Medhanie Alem. He sees the men in their splendid white robes and turbans, a large painting of Jesus on his cross over the altar. With his dark complexion and large dark eyes, he looked more like a youthful Ethiopian than a poor Jew. He remembers the smell of incense rising up in the air from a pair of giant censers, the chandeliers with their lit candles, the stone baptismal, the sounds of the drums and the *sitra*, the incantatory sounds of the chanted liturgy, and the clapping of hands.

The villa is completely silent apart from the sawing of the crickets, the soft *hush, hush* of the waves in the distance. The servants have long since returned to their village for the night. He is alone, completely alone with M. So often she has come into his room to watch him sleep, turning on the light, stealing not just his sleep but something more precious with her avid gaze, her grasping hands, her pleas. She has used him up, prodding and poking at his flesh as if she wanted to possess his youth, his beauty, his life. He has been her chattel, her sex slave. She has forced him to lie on her thin body, to penetrate her with his tongue, his hands. Now she has discarded him, sloughing him off like the old skin of a snake; she has humiliated him deeply, wiping out his existence, to the point that he no longer knows who he is.

He creeps quietly along the corridor, clinging close to the wall like a shadow. He walks silently across the living room and up the stone stairs and opens the door to her suite. Now he is the voyeur. He turns on the small lamp on her desk and quietly opens her shutters on the moonlit night. He lets the night invade her room with him. He stands by her bed and looks down at her, as she lies beneath the splendid blue iron bed-head. He watches her helpless sleep. Her mouth is half open, her breathing stertorous, a thin trickle of saliva in a corner of her lips.

He remembers watching Solo sleep quietly beside him and how smooth his dark, dewy skin was. How touching he was in his defenselessness. M.'s body tilts to one side slightly, the angular lines, the thrust of the hip bone, the parted thin legs visible beneath the white sheet. Her body looks dislocated, lifeless, caught up in this artificially created little death.

He remembers her floating into the café, that other woman with the famous face, whom he recognized with such a thrill. He remembers the exciting, smoky sound of her masculine voice, his fear and his hope, the large, limpid eyes, full of sympathy. "I will help you," she had promised.

Now all her glamour has vanished. Without her elegant clothes, without the mask of her makeup—there are still traces of blue mascara around her eyes—without the hat to conceal the thin, greasy hair, without her emerald rings lying now in a tulip-shaped glass bowl by her bed, without the allure of her reputation, she looks simply old and ugly to him. He notices the brown spots on the sides of her face, the lines, the sharp, pointed nose, the thin lips, an unsightly gray hair on her chin. He would like to pluck it out.

He has glimpsed this many times before, but now he sees it all so clearly, as if under a magnifying glass. The chapped lips gape in an unseemly way. He sees the lined neck, the gray skin, the slump of the loose breasts she has made him hold. When he leans closer, he smells the breath that stinks of alcohol and bitterness. The bottle of sleeping pills and the half-empty vodka bottle are on the nightstand beside a glass, the rim stained with purple lipstick. She likes vodka, she says, because it has no taste, but perhaps she thinks you cannot smell it on her breath. She is mistaken.

The manuscript of her new book that she calls a novel is piled on her desk beside her typewriter, all 150 pages, carefully edited by him. Her books are often short, hardly novels, rather novelettes, he thinks, but nobody seems to mind. They print them in large print with frequent white spaces, her name enough to sell them, apparently.

He wonders if her work will last. Correcting her repetitive prose, he has lost much of his admiration for her as an artist. Her books have been overrated, in his opinion; even her early ones don't have the allure they had once, now that he knows her so well. Her publishers and above all her publicists have done good work for her. The strength of one or two successful short books has carried all the rest. Fame is mostly a game of luck, it seems to him, an elusive whip-poor-will that may or may not last. Certainly she can no longer write anything with the energy of her early years. Without his corrections he is certain her editor would turn down the book that lies stacked on the desk.

XXII

As HE STANDS THERE AT HER BEDROOM WINDOW ASKING HIM-
self if he is capable of this, he becomes aware that the sun is
beginning to rise, the edges of the horizon stained pink above
the sea. The night is almost gone. He must decide fast. Soon
the couple will arrive from Abbiadori to start work.

His head is filled with the voice that has come back to record his actions. He is Dawit, a young man with large dark
eyes, in a fine linen shirt and navy linen trousers with a gold
cross around his neck, standing at the window, and he is also
someone else, someone unknown, watching himself. He tries
to concentrate on the task at hand, but extraneous thoughts
float through his mind as he stands there. He wonders why
the desk was built as a long plank of shining wood without
drawers, which would have been useful in a room of this
kind, and why, indeed, M. had this villa built on the side of
such a steep hill, though obviously it was for the view that lies
before him, in the first light of day: the splendid sweep of the
half-moon-shaped bay.

Then he turns his back on the view and looks at her, still
sleeping so soundly while he has been awake all night. For
her he has been just a small link in what was probably a long

chain of young lover-cum-secretaries, available young men who would do her bidding and whom she has taken into her house and used for a while. She has decided to banish him and will forget him fast, he is certain. In the end he has meant little to her. She intends to go on with her life, her successful career, and forget him completely. Perhaps she hopes that he will be banished far from her sight, sent back to his homeland, his cell.

He remembers standing with the chain in his hands; the guard entering his room. In the end it had been a simple choice, one that soldiers make every day: their own life or that of another. It is an act many men commit again and again in battle. Birth and death; one unimportant, useless life lost for the good of many.

He picks up her emerald rings from the bowl and slips them onto his two pinkies. Afterward, it is this action that he will find the most incomprehensible, the theft of a few stones, though what follows is surely stranger. He lifts the glass on the blue bedside table and mixes the vodka left in the bottle with the rest of the sleeping pills, stirs them together. He wants to fill her with this liquid, to invade her being just as she has invaded his. He will give her everlasting sleep, in return for having so often stolen his. Also, despite everything, he is loath to make this elderly woman, who has loved him in her way, suffer.

He sits down by her side on the bed and gently pushes her over onto her back. Then he props her up, so that her mouth opens wider, and he pours the liquid easily into her throat. She wakes immediately, of course, which he realizes he should have known she would do. What is he thinking? What is he doing? He can see the liquid is not going down her throat. She is trying to sit up and spit it out, but he holds her down, pushing against her chest, her head. His efforts are misdirected. She spits out the liquid and thrusts the glass away from her mouth, clawing at his hand with her nails, thrusting it away from her, trying to sit up. She reaches back to hang on to the iron bed-head to draw herself up, and for a moment he thinks the whole thing will crash down and kill them both.

He draws back from her, stands up, and pushes on the bed-head to keep it upright. He hesitates, afraid of her now that she is awake and protesting so violently, shouting at him, "What are you doing?" He is so used to doing her bidding, obeying her orders, trying always to please. How can he do this to her, this woman who has been his benefactor? But he thrusts her back against the pillows roughly, bending over her and placing one hand in the middle of her chest, where the guard had thrust the gun into his mother's. He wrenches her fingers from the iron bed-head behind her and recommences uselessly trying to force as much of the liquid as he can down her throat, jamming the glass between her yellowed, nicotine-stained teeth. Sputtering and choking, beating the glass away, so that much of the alcohol is soaked up by her white silk nightgown, the white lace pillow slip, she shouts at him again—"Get away from me!"—in groggy surprise, her voice so loud and forceful it frightens him.

"I'm trying to make this easy for you," he says absurdly, trying to justify himself, but she continues to struggle with him, screams loudly for help, and beats away the glass so that it flies onto the tiled floor, where it shatters. For a moment he wonders if he should abandon everything, give himself up to her, not so much out of fear but out of horror at what he is doing and repulsion for himself. At the same time, he knows that he cannot retreat now. It is too late.

Instead, he rips the cord from her white silk robe, sits behind her, and slips it around her neck. "For God's sake!" she cries out, tugging at the cord with both her hands, arching her back and kicking. He holds on and pulls even harder with all his force, dragging her head and neck back against his own body, as he had with his chain on the guard's neck, but now his strength seems to fail him with this weak white woman. He feels so feeble, exhausted, and unable to hurt an elderly woman who has given him back his life. She yanks the cord away from her neck, turning and kicking out at him brutally, thrusting at his sex with her knee and thrashing wildly around with her arms on the bed, and for a moment he feels he will not have the strength to hold her.

Driven now more by her violence than his own, remembering the electrodes on his genitals, trying to protect himself from her fury, he fights back. He is overtaken by some force that seems outside of himself, like the voice that speaks in his head. Watching himself from afar, he tightens the cord again and pulls so tightly that she cannot slip her fingers under it. Her hands give way, and he pulls tighter and tighter. She makes a strangled, gurgling sound, murmurs a name, as he, with as much pleasure as he had with the guard, listens to her gasp for breath before her long, bony body sinks down limply before him, back onto the soft white pillows behind her head.

White on white. Is she dead? For a moment he thinks he sees her flat chest rise and fall beneath the white gown. Is she just pretending, waiting for the moment to strike out at him like a snake? He cannot bring himself to touch her body, to feel her pulse.

At the same time, he is aware that the light is brighter, the sky whitening. He must hurry. He must make a plan. The couple must not find her lying here. He forces himself to put his fingers around her wrist, where he feels a faint flicker of a pulse that vanishes at his touch. He knows what he must do. He picks up the keys for the boat. Trembling, he forces himself to slip his hands under her and lift her long body in his arms with one strong sweep. She is surprisingly light. Her head falls back over his arm, and he recalls coming to her villa for the first time, and how in his excitement at the beauty of the place he had extravagantly swept her up and carried her over the threshold like a new bride. How heavy she had felt to him then.

Now he carries her easily down the corridor and pushes open the front door, lifting the latch with one hand. They go up the stone steps of the path, climbing the hill to the car. As he strides fast away from her house, he realizes he has grown strong and she weak in his time here. She has fed him and taken care of him, and now he has ended her life.

He wants desperately to lie down, to sleep, to forget. He is utterly exhausted after his battle with her on the bed. He is distracted again, too, noticing absurd things, the *amanti del sole* drooping and in need of water, the sky a faint pink. He must get her away from here. He manages to open the door to the white car and slips her onto the black leather seat. Her head falls back, but propped up, she looks almost alive. He cannot bear to look at her white face. He concentrates on the road before him in the faint dawn light, driving fast down to the hotel at Cala di Volpe.

He remembers her telling him about the place for the first time. He hears her hoarse voice saying, "Yes. It means the Bay of Foxes." Now he is the fox running from death.

XXIII

_____

THEY DRIVE TOGETHER IN THE WHITE JAGUAR, GOING DOWN to the glittering bay below as they have so many times. He parks in the hotel parking lot and sits a moment under the eucalyptus trees. He looks around the shadowy place, remembers the happy times when they have come here together when he delighted in her wit and her gaiety. He hears her laugh and say, "Everything reminds you of Ethiopia!" He cannot move, has no desire to go on, but as he sees no one about he forces himself to get out and lift her out of the car. Her head falls back against his arm, her legs dangle limply, but he cannot look at her face. He can only hope that if anyone notices them they might think she is sleeping or drunk or he is gallantly carrying his love to their boat.

Fortunately, at that early hour of the morning, there seems to be no one around yet. The guests, surely, must all be sleeping soundly after the revels of the night in their elegant hotel suites. None of the staff seems to be about yet, either, though he sees lights in the basement kitchens of the hotel and hears voices as he goes quickly along the quay.

He hears footsteps. Someone is coming along the quay behind him. Quickly he steps back into the shadows of an alleyway with his burden and waits, his heart drumming, as the man goes past. He watches as one of the staff stands smoking a cigarette in the dawn light, a bloody apron tied around his waist. The man stretches and then goes back into the kitchen below.

Almost running now along the quay, he reaches the motorboat tied up in the harbor with all the others, and drops her body down on the cushions. He has another thought, goes back along the quay, and picks up a length of heavy mooring chain.

By the first light of day, with the moon still a pale face peering at him from the sky, not another boat in sight on the sea, he unties the motorboat and steers it slowly and quietly out of the harbor, going across the calm, milky waters, using only the oars with a soft lapping sound, trying not to make any other noise or call attention to the boat. Not until he is farther out does he start the engine. He plans to take her to the place she loved, off the island of Mortorio, in water deep enough to hide her body. He remembers how she had said she would like to be buried there or rather left to sink down into the sea. Well, she will have her wish. He hears her saying, "Terrifyingly happy." Had she known then what might happen?

He goes fast now across the calm, clear sea, toward the island, stopping where the water seems deep enough, turning a dark blue here. In the glare of the rising sun, he ties the heavy chain tightly three times around her thin body. He looks down at her for the last time, brushing her hair gently from her face, and then, with a heave, his breath going from him as though it were he who will enter the water, he tips the chained body over the gunwale. He continues to hold his breath, watching as M.'s white gown fills with air and bubbles up, the white hair spreading out in the water, as though she were reluctant after all to sink down into the sea.

He sits for a while, watching the surface anxiously as the boat bobs in the calm sea. He peers down into the blue water but can see nothing. He wonders if the body has been pulled down into the very depths, if the knot he has tied with the chain will hold. Where is she resting?

On an impulse, he decides to dive into the water to make sure the chained body has gone down into the depths and lies securely on the sandy bottom. He wants to see her resting place. He pulls off his shirt, trousers, and underwear, stands naked on the side of the boat, fills his lungs with air, and dives into the water, going through the rays of sun into the depths of the blue sea, down and down. He sees a shape he thinks might be the body, but it is a large gray fish that swims like a bat flying through water, with wide wings and a kite tail. A stingray. He goes deeper but is not able to see the body. It seems to have vanished. He is confused in this strange, silent world of blue water, with only an occasional bright fish, flashing its round eye at him. He swims around trying to find M. down there in the depths. He panics, going deeper and deeper, his lungs bursting, it seems, as they did in the torture sessions in the prison, his head and shoulders held down in the filthy water. He tries desperately to follow her body to the watery depths, his head spinning. He must find her, make sure she has come to rest, whatever it costs him.

Now, swimming even deeper, he no longer feels the need to breathe. Instead he is filled with a strange, sleepy euphoria down there in the depths of the Bay of Foxes. He wants to keep on going down, to be with M. in her death, to entwine with her lifeless body in this world of the deep, as he was never able to do above. He feels he could enter her body as she had so wished he could, and this coupling would restore her to life.

It seems to him he hears someone calling him. It must be M. calling him down to lie beside her in her silent grave. Then he realizes it is his mother's voice. She is calling his name. "Dawit, Dawit, Dawit, my darling boy!" she calls out to him urgently. "Happy birthday!" she says, her voice chiming in his ears like a bell. It comes to him then that it is the sixth of September, his birthday. Of course. This day of all days is the day of his birth. Today he is twenty-one. The realization brings him back to his senses. Vaguely, at the back of his mind, he remembers hearing about the dangers of diving too deep, and the false sense of euphoria it can cause. He forces himself to give up his search and regain the surface, struggling up as fast as he can to the air, which never seems to come. Up and up he swims, desperate, his head spinning, until, gasping and sputtering, he emerges into the dazzling light.

Looking around in the early morning glare, he realizes that he has been down so long that the boat has drifted away from him in the current, or perhaps he has swum away from it in his fruitless search. Terrified, he looks around him, searching for the boat in the dazzle and gleam of white light. He can hardly see, his eyes smarting from his search through salty water. Around him there is nothing but clear blue sea. Then he catches a glimpse of something bobbing in the distance. At first he fears it might be M.'s body in its white shroud and chains. Then he spots the wooden trim of the gunwale and realizes it is the white boat, faintly visible. Wildly, he strikes out, terrified it will drift away, leaving him to drown, his body going down into the depths with M.'s on this day of his birth. He is already exhausted from his night of vigil, his struggle with M., and winded from his deep dive. He is unable to swim fast. He is drifting farther and farther away, carried by the current from the boat.

With a final effort, thinking of his mother's beautiful face and her loving gaze, he manages to strike out again and reach the boat. He flings an arm up to cling to the side, realizing then that he has not let the ladder down and will have to hoist himself up with his exhausted arms. He has no strength left. His head spins; his limbs are heavy. He thinks of all the stories he has heard of people in this predicament, swimming around and around a boat until they are so exhausted they drown. He feels the little strength he has left quitting his body, but he hangs on to the side of the boat with one hand, trying to gather enough energy, thinking of his mother's face, her dark, bright eyes looking at him so lovingly.

Hand over hand, he manages to get himself to the back of the boat, which is lower in the water and where the motor lies. Taking hold of the motor with a heave and a final effort, he manages to hoist himself up and fall into the boat, scraping the skin of his bare stomach. He falls exhausted, scratched, and bleeding, unable to move, lying flat on the cushions where M.'s body had lain. He forces himself to put his clothes back on, start the motor, and return the boat to the docks. There he ties it to the quay. Luck is still with him, and he sees no one about as he slips along the dock and back into the white car.

As he drives up the hill to the villa, images continue to come to him. He sees the body coming loose from its chains, floating up to the surface, and some fisherman hauling it up from the sea. Perhaps the traces of alcohol and sleeping pills he had forced down M.'s throat will cause it to be taken for a suicide if the body is found. He sees the body slowly decaying, the blue water of the whole bay gradually becoming murky, flecked with gray skin and bones, contaminated with death, M.'s death. Will the skin slowly peel from the thigh? Will a white thigh bone be caught in some swimmer's hair? He shudders. She died, he tells himself, not unlike Virginia Woolf floating down through the waters of the Ouse with stones in her pockets, surely a fitting death for a writer.

XXIV

O N   E N T E R I N G   T H E   H O U S E ,   H E   F O R C E S   H I M S E L F   T O   G O   B A C K
into M.'s room. For a second, faced by the sight of the disorderly bed, the rumpled sheets, the shattered glass, he feels his legs will give way. *He must clean up the room.* It is after nine o'clock, and the couple will soon be here.

The voice is back in his head. Feverishly, he gets a broom from the kitchen and sweeps up the shattered glass, pushing the pieces carelessly under the bed, throwing the blue bedcover with its bright embroidered flowers over the rumpled sheets. He catches a glimpse of himself in the bathroom mirror and realizes he has blood all over his shirt from his climb back into the boat. He is frantically changing his shirt into one of M.'s in her gray-tiled bathroom when he hears the couple arriving in their car. Soon Adrianna is singing gaily in the kitchen. He takes a great gulp of air, as if about to dive down again into the depths, and enters the blue-and-white-tiled kitchen.

Without wishing the couple a good morning, he announces that the signora has had to leave for a while. She asked him to let them know.

"But the signora always stays through September!" Adrianna exclaims, turning from the stove toward him. She clasps her hands together with disappointment and surprise. Michelino just stands there in the middle of the room, frowning at Dawit with concern.

"Something came up. She may be back sooner," Dawit says uncertainly. He feels unsteady on his feet, as though he is still in the boat, which is rocking beneath him. He can hardly see the couple. They sway before him alarmingly, and he is obliged to steady himself against the blue-and-white-tiled counter. His eyes smart from the saltwater and sun. He desperately wants them to leave, so that he can lie down and sleep. But they linger on, reluctant to go, staring at him, looking concerned. Adrianna asks him if he is ill, his eyes look red. The signore has not slept well?

He puts his hands to his eyes, tells her she's right, and attempts a smile. Clearly they want more information. They look so crestfallen and, it occurs to him, almost certainly have not yet been paid for their work this summer.

He claps his hand to his forehead in a dramatic gesture and says, "Oh! I almost forgot. The signora left something for you, a little bonus, after all your hard work." He goes into the living room, where the stack of money M. had left to get him off the island remains. Without counting it, he sweeps it up off the table, goes back into the kitchen, and thrusts the pile into Michelino's hands. "Here, this is what she left for you," he says. While Michelino looks down at the pile of bills in his hands, Dawit tells the couple M. had said they must take a week off. They deserve a little holiday. They must leave now. He is frantic to be alone, to sleep.

"Are you certain?" Michelino says, looking at Dawit, puzzled. "We'd be happy to work. We always work through September in the French signora's villa."

"No, no, I'll be fine alone for a week," Dawit says.

Michelino looks into his face and then back at the stack of bills in his hands. He is too polite to count them. "Are you quite sure?" he asks again, suspiciously. "The signora doesn't usually pay us until the end of September."

Adrianna says something to Michelino in the Sardinian dialect that Dawit does not understand. Then she says in Italian, "If the signore needs anything he can just give us a ring. He has our number," in a bright, cheerful voice as she picks up her cream handbag from the kitchen table. She takes the money from Michelino—clearly she is the one who manages the finances—and puts it away in her bag. "Come on, Miche," she says gaily and takes him by his hand. He follows her lead reluctantly, looking back over his shoulder at Dawit, who wonders what he is thinking and what he might say if anyone inquired about M.'s whereabouts. Do they believe his story? Or is it just convenient to pretend to? Are they too polite to ask any more questions? They go out the door, with Adrianna leading the way, waving happily, reminding Dawit to ring if he needs their help, and Michelino giving a worried backward glance at the house he has always tended so carefully.

XXV

HE GOES INTO HIS BATHROOM AND PEELS OFF ALL HIS CLOTHES fast. He turns on the shower tap hard and has a long, hot shower, washing the scrapes on his stomach with soap, scrubbing himself all over. Then he wraps himself in a toweling robe and climbs into his bed. He lies back shivering despite the hot water, the thick robe, the heat of the day. His teeth clack, and he cannot still his trembling body. His heart beats so fast it seems to shake the bed. He rises again to cover himself with a heavy blanket, but the long dive to the depths, the endless swim in the sea, the events of the entire night without sleep, have all chilled him through and through. He has never felt so tired in his whole life.

Eventually he falls into a deep and undisturbed sleep. He sleeps and sleeps. When he wakes it is late afternoon, and he realizes he has eaten nothing since he and M. had eaten their silent meal the evening before. He is now strangely calm and completely famished. It is his birthday, after all. An important birthday. He prepares a huge feast, using everything he finds in the refrigerator. He scrambles eggs and lays out all the prosciutto, figs, cheese, the flat bread and yogurt and honey for dessert. He goes into the cellar and takes out a bottle and then opens the champagne, carrying everything on a tray out onto the terrace, where he sits with his feet up, surveying the beauty of the bay in the twilight. He savors each morsel with deep satisfaction, as though he has never eaten enough in his life before, gluttonously consuming all the flat bread with honey, sucking the sweetness from the tips of his fingers. He drinks the entire bottle of champagne.

He drifts alone through the empty rooms as night falls, listening to the hollow sound of his footsteps. *This is my domain now*, he thinks. He is free to do exactly as he wishes for the first time in his life, though, in a way, he feels as he did on his escape from prison. He is light-headed, floating through the beautiful twilit rooms as though he were still underwater. He swims across the polished floors, hardly touching the ground, switching on lights, opening closets, drawers, exploring all the secret spaces of the house, ferreting through all of M.'s intimate things, her papers, her clothes, her jewelry. He opens her safe. He knows the combination, which, always forgetful of numbers, she has written down in her address book. Besides, he has seen her open it many times and unlike her he has a good memory for numbers. He counts the money, a considerable sum, and then puts it back.

He is drawn back into her bedroom. He switches on the bedside lamp and stares at the empty bed with its bright embroidered counterpane. He opens up her closet, pulls out certain garments he has seen her wear, and throws them on the bed. He tries on the ones she wore that he admired the most: a velvet jacket in a deep midnight blue, with a seahorse pin in diamonds on the lapel, a pair of black tailored pants, crocodile shoes in black with little tassels. He stands erect before the mirror in her bathroom. He angles a maroon brimmed hat rakishly, as M. once did, and smiles at his reflection, with a glimmer of his old arrogance in his large eyes. He places a Gitane in her tortoiseshell cigarette holder, draws in the smoke, and puffs it at his reflection in the mirror. He says to himself in her hoarse voice, "Take anything you want, darling. It's all yours now."

"Beautiful," he says. "You look beautiful!" and he gives himself a kiss in the mirror.

As night falls, he pours himself a stiff vodka and tonic, drinks it stretched out luxuriously in her armchair, looking over the beautiful bay in the moonlight. He sits at the grand piano in the living room and plays until late that night, playing her favorite pieces, the Debussy she loved. "I'm playing this for you, M.," he says.

XXVI

HE AWAKES WITH A HEADACHE, HIS MOUTH DRY, BUT HE DRAGS himself from his bed. He must maintain the same rhythm to his days. He must not take to his bed. He runs barefoot as usual down to the Piccolo Pevero. He goes on through the calm, sheltered area with its low shrubs and white sand, over the hill to the next beach, panting and hot, the sweat running down his back, but he cannot plunge back in the water. He stands at the edge of the sea, shading his eyes from the glare. The clear emerald water now seems dangerous to him. Somewhere down there, M.'s body lurks. He fears he may meet some part of her if he swims. She is waiting for him. He imagines a hand reaching up for his neck, to pull him under, a foot springing out to kick at his most intimate parts, as she had done on the bed, her white hair veiling his face, blinding him. He turns away and runs fast back to the villa.

He showers and forces himself to sit at her desk in her bedroom, but what he thinks of now is Enrico. He wants desperately to talk to him. His hand goes to the black telephone on the desk, but it stops in midair. He knows he is not to call him. He cannot speak to him over the telephone. He rises and walks back and forth in the room, looks at his watch.

It is near noon. He considers going to the tennis club, but he doesn't trust himself to speak to Enrico in person. He knows Enrico will be leaving for Rome soon. He needs to talk to him, at least to say good-bye. But what can he say? He does not want to lie to him. He's not sure he is able to lie to him. He looks out the window at the bay and hears him saying, "Lying is a lonely business, *amico mio*." Nor can he burden Enrico with the truth. Besides, thinking about it in the bright light of noon, he is not at all sure he can trust Enrico to be discreet. He imagines him telling someone, blurting the story out in a moment of sincerity. He is not a discreet man. He might even tell his wife, perhaps, whom, despite everything, Dawit knows Enrico loves. And to whom might the wife speak? Might she then pass on the news to her father, who could blast it across Italy? Dawit is not sure that Enrico wouldn't betray him without even meaning to. He decides silence is the only solution for the moment.

He sits down again and tries to concentrate on the work before him, but he is terribly distracted. He hears M. saying "an excellent secretary." He will be one indeed: his own. He forces himself to answer the letters that need to be answered in his neat hand. He finds the letter from the college in America and politely refuses the position. He pays the bills that are due, as he always does.

He even manages to work on her book, making further improvements freely now, rewriting many of the chapters. He moves the plot along faster, introduces more dialogue, heightens the drama.

But the thought that he can no longer speak to the one

person whom he cares about more than anyone else keeps coming back to him—a dreadful thought. If he cannot speak to Enrico, to whom will he be able to speak? To no one, he realizes. He is tormented by the desire to speak to someone, to tell someone what he has done. He is alone again in all this luxury, with the sun shining, the sea glittering before him, with the plumbago and the hibiscus blooming and the olive trees glinting silver in the sun—as alone as when he lay in his prison cell.

When the phone rings, he startles, and then lets it ring. When he can no longer bear the ringing, feels obliged to answer, he tells the man who asks for her that M. is not there. He is not sure when she will be back. He leaves it at that.

In the afternoon he makes a point of taking the Jaguar out and going into the bank in Porto Cervo to say a few words to the bank manager, a young, handsome, neat Sardinian, in his dark linen suit, sitting in his little orange office. Dawit knows him quite well, as he would go there to draw money for M. or for himself. His own money transfer has not been stopped, he is relieved to see.

The bank manager inquires politely after M. He hesitates a moment, and then tells the man she has gone to her house in Switzerland. He has already calculated that the three houses will come in handy. He has all the keys. M. drifted from one to the other as well as traveling to other places for her work or pleasure. It was always hard to pin her down.

He goes to the small post office in the town with his checkbook and writes out a large check, standing at the high counter under the window. He will send it to Asfa with a little note: "Please go to church for me and say the prayer for the dead," he writes. There is no need to explain. Asfa will assume he is thinking of his dead parents. Indeed, he does think more and more of them.

As he stands in the post office writing out the note on the dusty wooden counter, he remembers a moment with his father. Dawit had met him during his holidays in Paris, where his father was staying at the Ethiopian Embassy near the Eiffel Tower. He must have been fourteen, an awkward age. It was one of the few times he had been on his own with his father. He was not used to talking to him alone. His mother was the one who made the conversation, asked the questions. His father told him he wanted to take him to see his favorite opera, an opera by Verdi: *Aida*. He had taken Dawit out to dinner beforehand in a famous restaurant not far from the opera house, a hushed place with deep red walls and red velvet curtains and chairs. His father spent the elaborate meal telling Dawit about the plot of the opera and how much he loved Verdi's music. Dawit had heard only something vague about an Ethiopian king and his daughter, who has been captured and made into a slave. He had not dared to say anything, but he would much have preferred to listen to his own music in his room. He was a Beatles fan as an adolescent, playing their records incessantly. "Here comes the sun," he would sing joyously, his mood suddenly shifting.

During the long opera he had sat restlessly at his father's side, hardly able to hide his boredom, moving around uncomfortably in his seat. He found the plot ridiculous. The large singer who played Aida, despite her spectacular voice, her tragic dilemma, did not stir him, other than into fits of giggles, which he had difficulty controlling. His father sat beside him, swaying his head from side to side to the rhythms of the music, conducting with one finger and humming along to the arias he loved particularly. "Celeste Aida," he hummed, much to Dawit's extreme embarrassment. He could see that his father was annoying his neighbors but seemed oblivious to their muttered comments. Dawit wanted alternately to giggle—the "celeste Aida," a large lady in a wig and bright blue caftan who tottered on tiny feet across the stage, seemed hardly divine to him—or to weep with embarrassment at his father's absurd antics.

During the first interval, his father asked him how he was enjoying the opera. "Isn't it fantastic? Have you ever heard anything so beautiful?" he said, and Dawit was obliged to shake his head and say he had never heard anything like it. Then he asked if he might have something to drink. His father bought him an exorbitantly expensive glass of champagne, his first, which he gulped down thirstily, the bubbles going up his nose. He remembers now, when the opera was finally over and they had walked outside, his father lingering in the street as though reluctant to leave, looking back at the ornate opera house lit up, with the blue of the night sky behind it. He put his arm around Dawit's shoulders and asked, "Will you remember this evening, Dawit?" He could only nod politely, looking down at the ground, embarrassed by this public embrace, hoping to forget the entire excruciating experience as soon as possible. His father had looked at him tenderly, standing there beside him in the street, the opera house behind them, as he said—Dawit can hear his voice now—"I know I'll remember being here with you to the end of my days."

Then Dawit writes out another check to help the famine-stricken people in his country, hoping it will reach them. As he drives back to the villa he wonders how long he will be able to take M.'s place and use her money as he thinks fit.

XXVII

WHEN M.'S EDITOR, GUSTAVE, CALLS ONE AFTERNOON IN LATE September, he startles Dawit, who is sitting at M.'s desk in her room looking over the bay. He has his feet up on the desk in her crocodile shoes and is contemplating the view, pencil in hand. Gustave tells him he's at the airport in Olbia. Is someone coming to pick him up? "She hasn't forgotten me, has she?" he asks. Dawit suddenly remembers that M. had spoken of this yearly visit to the island in late September. He has, indeed, completely forgotten about it.

He thinks fast how to handle this, but all he can come up with is, "No, no, of course not, she would never forget you."

"She's not ill, is she?" the editor asks.

"Oh, no, not ill!" Images of her face, her white hair, her white robe filling with air before sinking down through the water, come to Dawit vividly.

"Will you come and pick me up, then, or am I going to have to get a taxi?" Gustave says, beginning to sound annoyed.

"Of course, I'll be right there. I'm so sorry. A slight mix-up. Have some lunch," Dawit says, stumbling over his words. He is trembling, afraid his voice will betray his panic. What is he going to do? A mistake like this can be disastrous, he knows. How could he have been so absentminded? Why had he not called to put off the visit?

"Has she finished her book? Do you know?" Gustave asks.

"Oh, yes, it's finished," he can truthfully say with some assurance. "It's waiting for you to read," he says, staring at the manuscript, which is in a neat pile stacked up before him, typed up on M.'s old Olivetti. "Look, I'll be there as soon as I can. I'll find you in the restaurant?" Dawit says, attempting to sound businesslike, cheerful.

"You'll find me in the bar!" Gustave says. Dawit hopes the man is drunk by the time he arrives. From the look of him, the broken veins in his cheeks, he is probably a heavy drinker.

Thank God the house is tidy, Dawit thinks, looking around M.'s bedroom, as he picks up the telephone to call the couple in Abbiadori. He has kept it orderly, the bed neatly made, the clothes put away. Breathlessly, he tells them to come as soon as possible to get the guest room ready: "*Il signore Francese, un signore molto importante,*" he says and tells them to pick some flowers for the room, to get something special for dinner that night, a seafood platter, lobster if they can find it.

Then he races out of the house, goes up the hill, and gets into the Jaguar. He drives into Olbia as fast as he can, screeching along the winding road that hugs the coast, trying to make a plan. He sees the sea glittering on one side, distracting him with thoughts of M., and on the other, the shrub-covered hills. His mind is a jumble. He is shaking so much when he steps out of the car he can hardly walk into the airport. Why has he forgotten this visit? What is the matter with him? Has he lost his mind? His agitation increases with every step he takes, afraid he has lost the ability to think clearly, to protect himself. He has quickly fallen into a false sense of security, wandering around the empty rooms of the villa, sitting writing at her desk, talking to no one, pouring himself a first drink at seven, as M. had done. He has drunk too much of her vodka. Now he can hardly find his way through the airport. He is almost at the bar when he realizes that he is still wearing M.'s rings and quickly slips them into his pocket. A foolish mistake like that could cost him everything. He looks down at the black crocodile shoes and thinks he should have changed them.

Gustave has obviously been drinking while he waits and looks red-eyed, sitting slumped over at the bar, his tie loose, his blue linen suit crumpled. He looks up and smiles when he spots Dawit. After slapping Dawit on the back and telling him he's glad to see him, he follows him through the airport to the car and then falls asleep almost immediately, head back, mouth open, snoring. As Dawit takes the sharp curves along the winding road that follows the coastline, he glances at the heavy Frenchman, helpless in his deep sleep, his plump hands open at his sides. He recalls Gustave's proposal to use Dawit as a gift, a brown diamond, for his wife's birthday, as if he were a commodity, a stone, or rather a penis to be bought and sold. He thinks of the arrogance of these French intellectuals, their endless and pointless discussions of theoretical matters, their inaction. He sees himself tightening the loose tie on the thick throat and almost goes off the road on a steep curve. He must remain calm, make a sensible plan.

By the time they arrive at the villa, Dawit has thought of something. He carries Gustave's brown leather bag, which is ominously heavy, to the guest room. The couple have prepared it in haste, but the two single beds with their cream counterpanes are made up neatly. Everything is clean and orderly. A bunch of pink hibiscus in a round blue-and-white vase stands on the bedside table between the beds and beside the telephone.

"Well, this all looks very nice," Gustave says, apparently somewhat mollified, surveying the comfortable room with its two pretty blue headboards painted with sea scenes by an artist from the island. He opens the linen curtain and looks out on the garden behind the house, with its olive trees and blue plumbago tumbling down the terraces. His room does not look over the bay as Dawit's does, but it is cool and attractive and has its own yellow and-white-tiled bathroom. Dawit tells him to make himself at home, to settle in. He will bring him M.'s manuscript to read.

"Good idea," the editor says without much enthusiasm, lifting his suitcase and putting it on one of the beds, beginning to unpack.

Dawit says he has to pick up something at the shops for dinner. He'll be back soon. Will Gustave please answer the telephone if it rings? M. has said she will call this afternoon to see if he has arrived. Then he gives Gustave the manuscript of her novel, putting it on top of the dresser, and leaves him unpacking in the room.

He drives to the hotel at the bottom of the hill, goes to the phone booth, and telephones the villa. He waits, his mouth dry, his hands damp and shaking, for Gustave to pick up, which he eventually does.

"Gustave, darling, did you get there safely? So sorry to

miss you. I'm afraid I've been held up," he says in M.'s hoarse, quavering voice.

"Where on earth are you?" Gustave asks. "What has happened?"

"Oh, God, I can't go into it on the telephone. I'm in Switzerland. A problem in the house here. I'm going to try and get back as soon as possible. Make yourself at home. Help yourself to anything you want. Get Dawit to open the champagne. Have him chauffeur you. I'm sure he has already given you my manuscript."

"I'm reading it now," he says. "I look forward to seeing you, darling, and talking about it. Come soon," and Dawit hangs up the telephone, though he would like to hear what the editor has to say about the book, his book, he thinks.

XXVIII

HE DRIVES UP THE STEEP HILL TO THE VILLA STILL SHAKING.
The night in M.'s room comes to him vividly. The moment
that he cannot fathom is how he was able to take the rings
from the bowl and slip them so easily onto his fingers. Everything followed from that. He recalls his mad scheme to drug
her to death with her own medicine, using the vodka and
sleeping pills. He hears again the glass shattering on the floor
and sees her thin white arms thrashing about wildly, feels her
kick out at him.

How is he going to care for this unwanted guest for several days, with these images coming to his mind? What will
he tell him? He fears saying something that will give himself away. He determines to bring out the champagne immediately, to get Gustave drinking again. Perhaps he himself
needs a drink, too.

But Gustave has other things in mind. He is waiting for
him on the terrace. He has changed into his navy blue swimming trunks, which look new and shiny. His considerable
stomach bulges under a light blue T-shirt. He tells Dawit he
wants to get some exercise before dinner. The sea looks wonderful, that clear blue water. He drank too much in the bar.

"This is such a gorgeous place, isn't it?" he says to Dawit, making a gesture toward the bay, where the sun is already low in the sky. Dawit just nods his head, speechless. Gustave says, "I can't think why M. would have left here just now. She usually loves September here, always says it's the best month, when the water is still warm but the crowds have left. Sometimes she even stays through October." He looks at Dawit as though he expects a response, but Dawit can only shrug his shoulders and sigh. "Could we take the boat out to the islands?" Gustave asks. He adds, "What's that island M. likes so much?"

"Mortorio?" Dawit says without thinking.

"That's it. Let's go there before it gets too dark and have a swim."

Dawit cannot think of anything to say. He considers pleading illness—indeed, he feels ill but realizes it would be unwise. Better to keep the man busy, even if he seems to have had the most diabolical idea. How can Dawit take him back to the place where he left M.?

He is obliged to drive the man down to the harbor and to walk along the quay as he did with M. in his arms in the dawn light. He has not been back here since her death, has carefully avoided the place, the boat. He is not even sure there are not traces of his blood on the boat's engine. The sun is beginning to set as it was rising that day, as he helps the portly editor into the boat. He unties the docking lines, unable to say a word, sunk into a reverie. Fortunately, Gustave, who is obviously not a boatman, seems to concentrate on the ride. Dawit sits in the stern of the boat, behind the editor, who sits in the middle, his back to Dawit, his plump hands spread out on each side of him to steady himself. He turns to smile at

Dawit benevolently, decked out in his expensive striped bathing trunks, a thick Hermès towel around his red neck. Dawit starts up the engine without difficulty and looks across the water, the late afternoon sun a glare in his eyes, but what he keeps seeing is M.'s face in the sea, the floating white hair and the white nightdress that bubbled up as she sank down. He looks at the oars lying in the bottom of the boat and glances at Gustave's back, the roll of flesh protruding from his shirt as he hangs over the side of the boat, trailing plump fingers in the clear water.

"Such clear water," he repeats, as if to remind Dawit of his predicament, turning back to smile contentedly at Dawit, making him draw in a sharp breath, imagining the body coming loose from its heavy chains and floating up to the surface or even, having drifted into shallow water, becoming visible at the bottom of the clear sea.

The editor, to make matters worse, quizzes Dawit as he attempts to concentrate on the steering of the boat. He asks him about M.'s departure. When did she leave? he wants to know. Dawit stares across the water and tells him he had driven her into Olbia to catch her plane for Geneva a few weeks ago. He keeps things as vague as possible. "I left her in the evening at the airport," he feels he can safely say. "She had been in Sassari to do a reading and came back early," he says, telling as much truth as possible. Besides, the editor may have heard about the visit to Sassari, for all he knows.

"Did you know she was to do a reading in Sassari?" Dawit asks.

"First I heard about it," Gustave says, turning his head.

"Had you two quarreled or something?" Gustave asks

shrewdly, looking Dawit in the eye. "It surprises me she went off alone. She seemed so fond of you—I'd even use the word *besotted*. She seemed to want you always at her side," and he laughs his big laugh, which shakes his stomach like jelly.

"*Oh, mon Dieu, non!* We never quarrel. How could I? She has been so good to me. I'm very grateful," Dawit says quickly, and then realizes his words are too strong and do not sound sincere. Such phony dialogue, he would never put into a novel.

"I know how difficult and demanding she can be," Gustave says, taking the towel off and laying it down beside him in the boat. "She and I have had a few quarrels, I can tell you," he adds, glancing back at Dawit.

Dawit just stares across the sea and says, "Really?"

Gustave adds, "Certainly you have lasted much longer than the others."

"Others?" Dawit asks.

"Oh, God, yes. There have been a string of young, attractive men over the years, I'm sure you must know. None of them has lasted more than a few weeks, as I recall."

"Really?" Dawit says again, though he has certainly suspected as much.

"In my opinion you have been smart, helping her with her work, which I certainly hope she appreciates," Gustave says, turning toward Dawit with a grin.

Dawit continues to steer the boat to a spot as far from the place where he left her as possible, but he is not at all sure the body would not have drifted in the currents or even risen to the surface.

"This is a perfect spot for a swim. Shall we anchor?" Gustave suggests. Dawit says he will stay in the boat, he doesn't feel like swimming this evening. He has not been swimming since the night she died. He cannot get back in the water.

"Too bad. The water looks wonderful to me," Gustave says as he prepares to make a leap from the side of the boat, holding his nose like a child and landing with a large splash, shaking the boat dangerously. He comes up to the surface and lies on his back and kicks up a spray. He calls out to Dawit to join him.

"I think I'll just stay here. I've done enough swimming recently," Dawit says to Gustave, reaching for one of the oars, just in case.

XXIX

DAWIT WANTS ONLY TO BE ALONE, ABSORBED BY HIS OBSESSIVE thoughts, but now he has to entertain this thick-necked, large-bellied Frenchman, who is no fool. He decides to do it lavishly. While Gustave showers and dresses after his swim—Dawit can hear him singing lustily in the shower—Dawit goes into the kitchen and asks the couple to stay late and serve dinner. They have done the shopping for Dawit in haste and are now preparing a large platter of seafood for the hors d'oeuvres: oysters, clams, and grilled calamari. Adrianna is grilling lobster for the entrée, melting butter and stirring in lemon and parsley.

"This all looks fabulous," Dawit says, smiling at them, glad he has taken the trouble to ingratiate himself with the young couple. *"Che pranzo splendido!"* Dawit says to them.

The couple are obviously happy to be back in the house, working. Adrianna has brought a large glazed fruit pie from the excellent baker in Abbiadori, as well as lettuce and tomatoes for salad. He has them open the good champagne, put out nuts and olives. Fortunately, he has the key to the cellar and knows the combination on the lock of the safe. He considers these expenses legitimate ones, business expenses.

He looks at Adrianna and tells her to pin up her hair and

put on some makeup. He adjusts her apron, pulling it in at the waist and tying a bow at the back. He smiles at her and Michelino. *"Bellissima, la tua moglie,"* he says, thus complimenting both of them.

It is a beautiful, clear night, and Dawit has the couple open the shutters on the patio behind them. A fine white cloth covers the round stone table, the silver shimmers, and bougainvillea spills from a vase in the center. On one side lies the bay with its moonlit water and on the other, the patio with the dark purple bougainvillea climbing up the wall. The air is redolent with the fragrance of herbs.

"What a feast, absolutely delicious," Gustave says, looking up at the flushed Adrianna, who serves the dishes with a big smile.

"What do you think of M.'s latest?" Dawit asks the editor as he cracks a lobster claw. "Did you have a chance to read it this afternoon?"

"I did actually read the whole thing in a couple of hours. I started it and quite honestly and rather unexpectedly couldn't put it down. It's unusually readable for her. I think it's the best thing she's done in a long while."

"I'm so glad you think so," Dawit says with genuine pleasure, lowering his gaze, adding, "She will be delighted, I'm sure."

Gustave looks Dawit in the eye. "Have you read it as well?" he asks him.

"Oh, yes, a few times. We worked on it through the summer. In fact, I did a little editing," he says modestly, and grins at Gustave and then lowers his gaze.

Gustave smiles at him with complicity, and says, "I thought

you might have, actually. There is something quite different about the prose." He searches for the right word. "A youthfulness, perhaps?" Dawit smiles.

Gustave cracks another lobster claw, extracts the flesh, and dips it into the butter. He asks Dawit, "Would you have any thoughts for the title?"

Dawit thinks and says, "What about *Black Eyes, White Hair*?"

"Not bad," the editor says. "I like it."

The editor sips his champagne thoughtfully and says, "I don't know what your relationship with M. is exactly, and quite frankly it's none of my business, but between you and me, I think she's lucky to have met you. Her work has improved considerably since you've been with her. You're a good editor, and for all I know a good writer. I hope she can convince you to stay around."

"I intend to," Dawit says to the man and pours him another glass of M.'s excellent champagne.

XXX

DAWIT IS WOKEN IN THE NIGHT BY THE LIGHT. FOR A MOMENT, half asleep, he thinks M. is back in his room watching him sleep, as she did so often. He feels a presence near him, a hand on his shoulder. He is not dreaming; this is real. Someone is definitely standing over him, menacingly. Someone is shaking his shoulder insistently. He sits up shaking, certain M. has come back to wake him up once again, to haunt him. Instead, when he opens his eyes properly, he sees not M.'s gaunt figure or any specter but the very real and stout Gustave, who leans over him in his maroon-striped pajamas. He says irately, "There is some fellow on the phone by the name of Enrico, who insists on talking to you. I answered because I thought it might be M. calling at this ungodly hour."

"God, I'm so sorry," Dawit says, jumping out of bed, holding the sheet to cover his nakedness. He adds, grinning foolishly, "My tennis buddy."

"Well, he's certainly not talking about tennis! Hell of a time to call. Three in the morning, and I wouldn't have woken you, but he sounds rather upset, and the more I spoke, the more upset he got," Gustave says, looking suspiciously at Dawit.

Dawit apologizes again and begs the editor to go back to sleep.

Once he has left, shuffling across the tile floor in his leather slippers, Dawit picks up the telephone beside his bed, his hand shaking. It is indeed Enrico, shouting into the phone. "What the hell happened to you? What's going on? I haven't heard a word from you. You knew I was leaving. Why didn't you call? Why didn't you come to the tennis club? And in God's name who answered the phone?" Enrico says, slurring his words, sounding very drunk. There are voices around him, people talking. He must be in some bar in Rome.

"Nothing. Nobody. Nothing is going on. Look, I can't talk now. It's three in the morning. I'm sorry. I'll call you tomorrow and explain. Give me a number where I can call you, a time," he says. He doesn't want to implicate Enrico, and he is not at all certain that the editor is not listening in to this call, would not be able to understand Enrico's Italian. He has not heard the receiver being replaced.

Enrico gives him his number at his office and tells Dawit to call around ten the next morning. "I'm sorry I woke your *guest*," Enrico says, his voice heavy with irony.

"It's M.'s editor, who is visiting," Dawit says in a low voice.

"Oh, really? Well, go back to bed. Go back to your sweet sleep," Enrico says irately.

But Dawit cannot sleep, afraid Gustave has overheard and might be growing suspicious. He leaves the house before dawn. He runs down to the Piccolo Pevero, lies on the sand in the faint light, staring up at the sky. He wants to go to Rome to find Enrico and talk to him. He needs to talk to someone frankly, to tell someone what he has done. Who else can he speak to, whatever the risk?

He calls Enrico from the hotel, after his run, and says, "Look, I've missed you terribly, but I can't talk about it over the phone. You'll understand when I explain. I'll come to Rome, if you can find time to see me, somewhere I can stay." He is beginning to feel Rome might be a safer place for him. "Can you find me somewhere to stay that won't cost a fortune for a few days?"

"Of course, no problem. You can stay at my brother-in-law's pied-à-terre for free. He's away, and it's not far from our apartment near the Piazza di Spagna. It's very small but it has a little terrace and a great view."

"Are you sure he wouldn't mind?"

"Not at all. They have so many of those millions. He's got about ten houses," he says, laughing. Dawit imagines Enrico lifting his beautiful hands in the air and shaking out the fingers like leaves on a tree to indicate the millions. "I can't wait to see you. I've missed you terribly. I'm sorry I called so late. Who was that man I spoke to? He sounded rather angry."

"Oh, I told you, just M.'s editor from Paris who has been staying in the villa."

"I see. Well, let me know just as soon as you have your ticket. Come soon," Enrico says.

"I have so much to tell you," Dawit says. "I'm going to come as soon as possible."

XXXI

GUSTAVE RISES LATE AND OVER BREAKFAST ANNOUNCES, to Dawit's relief, that he will be leaving today if Dawit can get him on a plane to Paris and to the airport on time. "There's no point to wait around for M.'s return. I want to get this book into production as soon as possible. Tell her if she calls, will you, that we want to rush it through? We can talk about the contract later," he says to Dawit, who nods his head and immediately says he'd be happy to make the arrangements.

Gustave looks at him. "I think we'll see if we can get it out by Christmas."

Dawit says, "Really, so soon!" then smiles and says he's sure M. will be thrilled.

Gustave looks at him from the sides of his shrewd blue-gray eyes and says, "If you hear anything from her, let me know, will you? I'm a little concerned, quite frankly. There is something strange going on, don't you think? I can't believe she missed my visit like this. I've been coming here at the same time for years. Was she drinking more than usual when she left, did you notice?"

Dawit thinks about what to say. "Perhaps, though it's hard

for me to say. She certainly likes her vodka in the evening, doesn't she?" he says cautiously, smiling.

"Was she depressed, do you think, when you drove her to the airport?"

Dawit considers. "She did seem rather down, but I thought it was because she had finished the book—a sort of letdown after the fact, postpartum depression—you know?"

"But she should be happy. It's very good," Gustave says, looking doubtfully at Dawit, who has the distinct impression he has divined the whole story. Will he go straight to the police on his arrival in Paris? He's quite sure the man will do whatever is in his own interest.

Dawit adds, soothingly, "I'm sure she'll call you soon. She admires you tremendously, and your opinion is so important to her."

"Good," Gustave says and smiles.

"Now let me get on the telephone for you. Do you mind going via Rome or Milan?" Dawit asks.

"Not at all, just get me on a plane," Gusave says. Obviously he is in as much of a hurry to leave as Dawit is to see him go.

Dawit rises fast from the breakfast table and goes down the steps into the living room. He feels Gustave watching him as he crosses the living room floor in his elegant linen pants and white linen shirt. Perhaps he should not have worn the new, elegant clothes M. had bought him. He wonders what the editor is really thinking and what he is deciding to do. Why is he in such a rush to return to Paris? Is he going there in order to call the police? Does he really think M. might have committed suicide? Surely he knows her well enough to realize she would never do something of that kind. Gone off on a drunken spree? Or does he suspect Dawit of murdering her?

He makes the necessary calls, gets the editor scheduled for a plane that afternoon, and carries his brown leather bag to the car. He drives him back to the airport, all in virtual silence, Dawit concentrating on the road.

"Just drop me off," the editor says, but Dawit feels obliged to park the car and accompany him into the airport. He waves good-bye to the man at the gate with a huge surge of relief, though he is not at all sure what is on Gustave's mind or what will happen next. Afterward, he goes to the bar at the airport and buys himself a vodka and tonic. He's beginning to like the taste of the drink.

While he's at the airport he decides to book his own ticket, to leave the next day for Rome. He buys the ticket and then calls Enrico and tells him he's arriving the next day. He considers calling Gustave, too, later that evening, and speaking in M.'s voice, but he decides he may have to get rid of M. for good. It is time he stood in his own shoes, he thinks with a smile, looking down at the expensive soft shoes she'd bought him.

Instead, he decides to call Gustave himself and speak in his own voice later that night, when Gustave has arrived at his apartment in Paris.

He tells him he hasn't heard from M. He, too, is starting to worry. He informs him of his departure for Rome the next day. He says he will be staying with a friend. He'll give him the number when he gets there in case Gustave needs to reach him.

"Thanks so much for your excellent hospitality. You have been most helpful. Have a good time in Rome," Gustave says cordially and adds, "If I were you, I might think about an alibi, someone who knows where you were the night M. was last seen," and he hangs up the phone.

XXXII

HAVING SPENT A RESTLESS NIGHT, DAWIT WALKS THROUGH the empty rooms of the villa. He looks around him for the last time. He knows it must be the last time. How could he ever come back to this beautiful and terrible place?

He goes into M.'s room and stands at the window looking across the bay, then he closes the shutters above her desk. He is careful to leave all of her belongings exactly as she had left them, even her Olivetti on the desk under the window, her letters and bills in neat piles. He puts her emerald rings back into the tulip-shaped glass bowl by her bed. How could he even have imagined he would wear them? He opens the safe and takes out only what he thinks is a fair amount of money to pay the couple for all their work this summer, a considerable sum of lire. Then he closes the safe, wipes off his fingerprints. He packs his bag, taking only a few of the clothes M. had given him.

When the couple arrive that bright, sun-filled morning, he tells them he is leaving for Rome. "So soon," Adrianna exclaims, looking disappointed. They ask if the signora is coming back this autumn, and he says he doubts it. He hasn't heard from her for a while. He says good-bye to Adrianna in the big blue-and-white-tiled kitchen, giving her a kiss on her smooth, fragrant cheek. He tells her to take any food that is left in the refrigerator and asks her to close up the house and make sure all is safe.

"As we always do," she says proudly. She adds, "We do hope you will come back soon, signore," obviously sincere in her wish, and gives him an affectionate hug. "It's lovely here at Christmas. You can even come and stay with us if you like," she says generously.

He climbs the hill and takes a last look at the sweep of the beautiful bay, the sun sparkling on the water, standing there with Michelino—who has insisted on carrying his bag— beside him. He has asked Michelino to drive him to the airport in M.'s Jaguar and leave him there.

Inside the airport, he buys them both a cappuccino at the bar and thanks Michelino for all his help this summer. It has been a privilege getting to know the couple, he says truly. He gives Michelino the money, telling him M. has asked that he pay him.

Michelino takes the wad of lire and looks at Dawit somewhat dubiously "So much? The signora is very generous this year," he says, looking Dawit in the eyes. Obviously Dawit has given the couple much more than they usually get. He wonders if this was wise. Michelino hesitates a moment, seems on the point of saying something, but then he just gives Dawit a big smile, a hug, and thanks him. He wishes him good luck. He waves as Dawit leaves to catch his flight. Dawit wonders what they would say about him, if the police ever questioned the couple.

He sits in the airplane shifting restlessly in his seat all through the short flight, thinking about Enrico, what he will have to tell him, and how he might react. Enrico has given Dawit the address and telephone number of the apartment in Rome. He has told him to take a cab from the airport and meet him in the street near the Spanish Steps.

Dawit tries to imagine holding Enrico again in his arms, but what he sees is an Italian policeman waiting for him at the airport.

PART THREE

Rome

XXXIII

DAWIT WAITS FOR ENRICO ANXIOUSLY, WATCHING THE PEOPLE pass by in the Roman street, in the sunlight. It is still warm in late September, and the trees retain their leaves. He watches the people's faces and admires their elegance, and often, their beauty. They stare at him frankly, too. He has the impression that unlike the French, they really see him, looking him up and down. He wonders what they think about this tall, well-dressed Ethiopian in his fancy sunglasses. He has dressed up for Enrico, put on his smartest navy linen suit and Panama hat, pulled down slightly to one side.

He sees a group of Gypsies begging on the street corner. A young, thin girl with a dirty face, dressed in a long, bright skirt with little glittering pieces of metal embroidered on her blouse, beats a tambourine and dances, turning and lifting her arms, her skirt swaying. Dawit thinks of his mother dancing in the palace hall. The girl's little brother, who has the streaks of tears on his cheeks, reminds Dawit of Takla. He goes over and drops a bill in the hat they have left on the pavement, and the young girl smiles at him and picks up the little boy. "Say thank you to the nice signore," she tells him.

Dawit wonders how Asfa's family is getting on. He remembers Takla looking up at him with big eyes as he consumed his *pain au chocolat*, sitting on the floor, little legs before him. It seems to have happened long ago.

Now that he is here, safely in Rome, he is filled with a sudden exhilaration. Clearly, Gustave has not sent the police to pick him up, or not yet. He is overjoyed to have escaped Cala di Volpe, where something unspeakable has happened. He is excited to see Enrico, uplifted by the beauty of the city around him as he was driven through the streets: the long-stemmed pine trees, reaching up to the sky, the brief glimpses of the famous Roman monuments he recalls from the postcards his parents sent him from a trip they had made with the Emperor: the Colosseum, the Circus Maximus, Hadrian's Arch. He hears his mother say, *"Levavi oculos!"* How he feels her presence here!

Now he is standing on a narrow side street near the Spanish Steps. Everywhere he looks, history was made, Italian history, with all its ambiguity. He thinks of the efforts the Italians made to colonize his country and his countrymen's brave resistance: his grandfather's stories of the Battle of Adwa, where the Italians expected an easy conquest and instead suffered a humiliating defeat. How proud his grandfather was of the soldiers he had led as a very young man into battle. How ironic that Dawit should be here now.

He begins to fear that Enrico will not show up. What will he do? Why had they decided to meet on a street corner? He is almost giving up, deciding he will have to look for a hotel, when he sees Enrico walking toward him, hurrying through the crowd, the sunlight shining in his red-gold curls. He is in his shirtsleeves, his linen jacket over his arm, almost running, his face lit up with joy. He lifts one arm to wave gaily from a distance. "My God, you made it!" he says exuberantly, as though Dawit is the one who is late. He grins widely, kissing him on both cheeks effusively and once again. "You look wonderful to me," Enrico says, waving his fine hands in admiration. Dawit looks back at the round amber eyes, the long lashes, the straight nose, and thinks how beautiful he is. "I'm so pleased to see you," Dawit says, realizing just how much pleasure this man has given him, how this ordinary Italian, in no way remarkable, has filled his life, has become his sole source of sorrow and joy. At the same time, with Enrico beside him, he is aware of how terrified he is of losing him completely, afraid of how he will react to what Dawit feels he must tell him.

Enrico leads him down the street, opens the heavy wooden door to a palazzo, and goes before him into a cool courtyard, with plants in big earthenware jars. He holds Dawit in his arms, pushing him back against the ancient stone wall, pressing his lips against his. Dawit can feel Enrico's whole body trembling. "Come, quickly come," Enrico says. "I've missed you too much. I've been a dreadful grumpy husband and father without you," he says, then grabs Dawit by the wrist, wrenches his suitcase from him, and half drags him up the worn marble steps.

XXXIV

Inside the fourth-floor apartment, Enrico closes the door and leans against it, panting and laughing, holding Dawit's hand, pulling him close. He drops Dawit's leather bag to the floor with a groan. "God, you feel good to me," he says, running his hands all over Dawit's body, pressing himself against him. Dawit feels the warmth of Enrico's soft body. He would like to rest in his arms and tell him everything.

But Enrico has other things in mind. He strips Dawit's clothes off, first the linen jacket, then the shirt. He wants Dawit to take him here and now on the floor. He cannot wait, it has been too, too long, why has he not called? What has been going on? But Dawit resists. He pushes Enrico away, saying they must talk first, he has something he must tell him, must ask him, a big favor. He has come to him because he does not know whom else to ask.

They walk into the small living room, and Enrico strides across to open the French windows on the sunlight and the small terrace with its round earthenware pots and vines climbing up the wall. Dawit follows him into the light, draws in a great breath of delight. He looks down onto the Spanish Steps, the boat-shaped fountain below. "My God, what a view!" he says. Enrico stands beside him looking across Rome, throwing an arm around his shoulders. "My gift to you," Enrico says, then turns and kisses him.

How can Dawit tell him what has happened? How can he burden him with it all? He looks into Enrico's eyes with longing. Enrico puts his hands around Dawit's waist and drags them down his thighs. All he wants, it is clear, is to lie beside Dawit and have him enter his body. He says, "I've done nothing but think of you and that white room at the club, the most beautiful place in the world. Lovemaking will forever be filled with the sound of people swearing and tennis balls being hit!" he says, laughing.

Dawit tries to stall, to curb Enrico's ardor. He asks for a drink. Enrico brings him a tall glass of cool mineral water from the small kitchen that opens onto the living room. They sit side by side on the gray love seat, which looks out over the steps, but Enrico looks at Dawit, frowning, puzzled. He rubs the end of his pointed nose, sighs, and says, "So what is so urgent that you have to tell me first? What can I do for you? I'll do anything," holding his freckled hands like a basket and thrusting them forward, to convey the extent of his willingness.

Dawit doesn't know what to say.

"Do you need money? You can have all I've got," Enrico says extravagantly, throwing up both his white hands as though throwing money to the sky, and grinning. Dawit shakes his head. "No! No! Not money," he says angrily.

"Well, then what on earth is it ?" Enrico asks.

"That would be too simple," Dawit says bitterly and looks

out the window. He cannot ask this man for anything, he decides. He has made a mistake. "Look, forget it. I can't ask you for this. I can't drag you into this. It's all too, too sordid."

"But I *want* to help you. I can see you are in trouble. I feel for you, as I would for myself!" Enrico says, holding on to him, both hands on his arms, looking concerned, his ancient face filled with melancholy.

"I don't want your pity. I don't want anything from you, from anyone. Do you understand?" Dawit shouts, suddenly enraged. He should never have come here. He's tempted to get up and go. He stands up, looks wildly around the elegant room.

"Are you crazy? What is the matter with you?" Enrico says, getting up, holding him tightly, his arms around him, looking into his eyes. "Why didn't you call me right away? Did something happen with M. after my visit? You had a quarrel? It was my fault? She is jealous? She turned you out? What happened?"

Dawit twists free and walks back and forth. He cannot speak truthfully even to this man he loves, because he loves him. He cannot drag him into something that might be dangerous to him and his whole family, the loving wife, the small children. Why make them suffer, too? He says, "It's nothing, I keep telling you. Forget it. I cannot ask this of you." He feels in that moment that he has never before experienced such awful sadness. It is a physical sensation that takes hold of his whole body. He feels he cannot move, can hardly speak at all. A fog of suffering seems to come down over him, envelop him. His head throbs, his throat feels raw, his eyes prick with tears. He will have to tell him as little as possible. He slumps down on the sofa, leans forward, puts his aching head in his hands.

Enrico takes him by the arms and shakes him hard, forces him to look at him. He says, "So you're in big trouble, no? I feel it. I will help you. Tell me now, you must. You must let me help you!"

Dawit looks at him and says, "Will you lie for me?"

Enrico grins and slumps back against the gray cushions, his hair rumpled, the buttons on his blue shirt undone. He has a wonderfully expressive face. There is no one in the whole world as precious to him. Enrico draws his shoulders up and lifts his hands. He says, "Of course, with ease. We Italians are pretty good at lying when we have to. I'd say no one else was quite as good at it. We can also steal. Do you need any stealing?" He opens his eyes wide, grinning, and then, seeing Dawit's expression, he looks serious, draws him close. He says, "I would lie and steal for you, Dawit. What else do you want? Why do you have to even ask? You want me to lie for you to M.? But why would she believe me? Never mind, I'd do anything for you, surely you know?" and he drags his hands over Dawit's chest, his thighs, his sex. Like M., he cannot keep his hands off his body, Dawit thinks, annoyed. All they want from him is his youth, his young body.

He looks at Enrico's fine patrician face, one of ancient privilege. His ancestors have known nothing but privilege. He has never known real hardship, hunger, or thirst. People have always come to his aid. No one has ever beaten the soles of his feet, plunged his head and shoulders in filthy water, put electrodes on his sex. How can he possibly understand? He is not so sure what Enrico would do for him, not sure at all. Would he betray him?

He says, "If they ask you, will you say you spent the night with me? The night when you left the villa? The night when M. found us together. Will you simply say you met me in a bar, and we went together to the beach, that we spent the night together there?"

"If who asks me?" Enrico asks, looking at him warily, his gaze fluttering back and forth across the room, as though he were watching a game of tennis. His face looks a little green around the fine nose.

Dawit looks at him and says, "The police."

Enrico draws a breath sharply, looks out the window, and then looks at Dawit. He says, "I'll say whatever you want me to, but now just make love to me."

Dawit puts his hands into Enrico's soft russet curls, he runs them over his face, his lips, down his sweet body, as Enrico pulls off the rest of Dawit's clothes and his own and sinks down onto the carpet before him. Dawit kneels naked beside him, feels the gold fluff on his stomach, and buries his face in his chest. He strokes his pale skin, the curve of his spine as Enrico turns onto his side, offering himself up, waiting for Dawit to fill his body with his sex. But what Dawit sees stretched out before him is not Enrico but M., her white gown bubbling up and her chained body sinking down through the blue sea. As Enrico turns to him and tries to arouse him, taking his sex hungrily into his mouth, he sees himself diving from the side of the boat, plunging down in search of M.'s body, not this one beside him. His desire is gone, stolen. He has left it down there in the deep of the Sardinian sea, buried in the sand of the Bay of Foxes. M. has managed to rob him not only of his sleep but also of his desire.

He struggles to his feet, tears on his cheeks. All he can say, as he once did to M., is "I'm sorry, but I just can't." Enrico, who is lying curled up on the Persian carpet in the Roman flat, the hum of the ancient city coming to them through the open door like the sound of the sea, lets out a deep, sustained moan. He calls on his God, asking for mercy, as though he has committed a crime.

Dawit says in a sort of furor, "It was her life or mine. She would have destroyed me, crushed me like a cockroach!" and as he says this he sees the expression in Enrico's eyes, the look of complete terror.

Enrico rises up on his knees and presses his hands together as though praying, shaking his hands pressed together at Dawit. He says, "What are you saying? What on earth are you saying! What did you do to her?"

Dawit explodes, "For God's sake! How much blood has been spilled and for how many absurd reasons? What does it matter? Surely the life of one hungry child, the life of little Takla, was worth more than hers?"

Enrico, still on his knees, looks up at Dawit and opens his arms wide, shakes his hands, his head, his whole body. He says, "Who are we to decide who is to live and die?"

Dawit looks away and says, "There was no other way out."

"Don't tell me that! Don't tell me anything! I don't want you to tell me what happened! I don't want to know." He bends over, lowering his head to the floor, touching the carpet with his forehead, covering his ears as M. once covered her eyes. Then he gets up and starts frantically pulling on his clothes. He says, "I have to go. I have to leave immediately."

"Go, then! Go ahead! Get away from me!" Dawit says.

Enrico finishes dressing, sitting on the sofa to pull on his elegant Italian socks, his fine, well-polished though worn shoes. He says, "Look, I'll lie for you. I will, if they ask me, and you can stay here for as long as you like, but try for God's sake to keep my family out of this. I don't want their names blasted across the papers. Do you understand? I don't want my wife, my children, dragged into this. I'll try and call but I don't know when I'll be back. Just leave the key under the mat when you have to go," and he gets up and goes toward the door. With his hand on the doorknob, he turns and looks at Dawit and for one wild moment Dawit hopes he might come back, take him in his arms, or at least say good-bye, but he tells Dawit there is food in the fridge, to help himself, and sheets for the couch, which folds out into a bed.

Up to the last moment a gentleman, Dawit thinks, blinking back tears. Then Enrico looks once at Dawit, his sorrow written clearly all over his face. He says with his small, sad, ironic smile, "*Ciao, Dawit, buona fortuna.*" As the door clicks softly behind him, Dawit feels as if he has been cut off from everything and everybody with a sharp knife.

XXXV

DAWIT LIES BACK DOWN ON THE CARPET, HIS KNEES DRAWN up to his chest, as Enrico had done. He cannot stir. He can hardly breathe. His whole body aches as though he has been beaten once again. Hot and cold shivers run down his spine. He thinks he hears screams, glass shattering, the sound of boots coming near. Vaguely, he is aware that no one is screaming, but the telephone, the big black phone, which is on the counter between the living room and the open kitchen, is ringing and ringing. Finally, he manages to rouse himself and forces himself up from the floor where he has been lying curled up in a ball, beating the carpet with his fists as he would do the concrete in his cell. He picks up the receiver. At first he is not able to understand what the voice is saying, but eventually he realizes it is Gustave. "Can you hear me, for God's sake? Dawit, I'm asking you if you have seen the papers today."

Dawit says no, the last thing he thought of was to buy a paper today. He has just arrived in Rome.

"It's all over the French papers, and I imagine the Italian ones, too," Gustave says.

"What is?" Dawit says, trying to understand. He sits down on the sofa, still naked and shaking. All he can imagine is a picture of himself in the paper with the word MURDERER underneath. Gustave says impatiently, "M.'s disappearance, of course. The police are looking for her. Look, I gave them your address in Rome. I had to. I wanted to warn you."

"I see," Dawit says, already imagining himself once again in a small cell, this time for life. He is tempted to get up and walk out onto the terrace and throw himself down onto the famous steps below. He thinks of Keats and the house where he died, which is very near here, he has noticed on his arrival. He thinks of the photo he saw of Keats's death mask in a book. He, too, will die young in Rome, but without having lived or written any poems. What is there left to live for, in any case? What is the point of going on? *Get it over with*, he thinks.

But Gustave encouragingly says, "Look, don't worry. It's just a formality. Nothing is going to happen to you. I spoke to them very highly of you, of course, and of your relationship with M. Everything should be fine. Just tell them where you were the night she took off. Perhaps she'll turn up, and in the meantime, it's good for business: a lost author! Very good for business. It couldn't have been better if we'd made it up!" he says with a laugh. He does not sound particularly concerned about his lost author. Did he ever really care about M.? Was this simply a business arrangement? "We're going to get that book out as soon as we can. November, probably," Gustave says.

"I see," Dawit says. Why should he care? he would like to say. Gustave is thinking of his sales. These French intellectuals, for all their fancy talk, think about nothing but money in the end.

But Gustave surprises Dawit once again. He says in a concerned, fatherly way, "Call me as soon as you have spoken to the police. They may want you to stay on in Rome for a while. Can you stay where you are?"

"Yes, yes, I suppose so," Dawit says indifferently, looking out the window, all the charm of Rome fled.

"Do you have enough money? That's a fancy address you gave me," Gustave says.

Everyone seems to want to give him money all of a sudden, Dawit thinks, and cannot help smiling at the irony. "Money. Yes, I have plenty of money," Dawit says, without much interest. He presumes his large allowance will continue without M. there to stop it, and in any case what is he going to do with money? How is he going to go on living, totally alone? Will he ever see Enrico again? Will he betray him? How quickly he had fled out the door!

"Well, let me know if you need anything at all. And in the meantime, if you've nothing to do, I'd suggest you start writing something. You knew her better than anyone, you know," Gustave says.

XXXVI

THE POLICE ARRIVE THE NEXT MORNING. DAWIT HAS JUST come back to the apartment, having found a café nearby where he has had a cup of coffee with milk and a brioche. He had eaten nothing since he left Cala di Volpe the morning before, and he woke from fitful sleep on the fold-out couch, on Enrico's brother-in-law's elegant striped sheets, he presumed, realizing he was terribly hungry.

He had also bought the newspapers, both the French and the Italian ones. The headlines were more or less the same in French and Italian: "Famous French Writer Missing," they announced in large letters, with information about M.'s life and work. He shuffled from one paper, one language, to the next, hardly able to read the print or concentrate on the text that danced alarmingly before his eyes. He started reading one in French and then read another in Italian, the facts, the languages, everything jumbled in his mind, while he perched on a stool in the bar of the small café, people coming and going around him distractingly. Any loud noise terrifies him: the sound of the coffeemaker steaming milk almost made him fall to the floor. *Calm down, calm down, you'll get through this*, he told himself.

There was no photograph of him, and no use of the word

murder, but in one of the papers he did find a reference to an unnamed Ethiopian secretary who was staying with M. in her villa at Cala di Volpe and was presumably the last person to have seen her before she disappeared, though her editor and publisher was reported to have spoken to M. since then on the telephone. Had Gustave really believed him or was it convenient for him to pretend to? What does Gustave know and what does he care? Suddenly the whole struggle to go on with his life seemed absurd to him, and he was filled with a dead hopelessness. It was all too difficult. How could he bear his secret?

Now Dawit slowly ascends the worn, dark stairs, remembering the wild climb with Enrico the day before. He can still feel that hot, eager hand achingly in his. The voice is back in his head recounting his actions, and he realizes he is muttering to himself. He looks up and sees men waiting for him on the landing outside the apartment. There are two of them in dark suits, obviously policemen though not in uniform. He had hardly slept all night, repeatedly going over what he planned to say to them, but now that they are here he is tempted just to tell them everything. He wants desperately to unburden his heart of everything that Enrico has not wanted to bear. He imagines falling on his knees before them, bowing his head, and telling the whole sordid story.

The policemen are not as beautiful as Enrico had proclaimed all Roman police were, though the older one is elegant, with his cape draped over his shoulder and a supercilious air about his dark, lean face. The younger one is tall and heavy-set, with a thick black mustache and a red face. He is in the process of scratching himself in a delicate spot with no semblance of elegance at all. Perhaps it is this that stops Dawit from falling onto his knees before them. How can he tell this vulgar policeman what has happened? How could the man possibly understand? Instead of feeling contrite, he is suddenly filled with irrational loathing. The policeman's bushy mustache seems particularly hideous.

The older one, with somewhat lined, tanned skin and an intelligent gaze, appears to be in charge as far as Dawit can tell, though it is the younger one who wishes him a *"Buon giorno, signore"* and asks if they may come in, adding rather rudely that they have been waiting awhile, as though this is Dawit's fault. They have a few questions they want to ask him.

Dawit apologizes, asks them please to follow him, and lets them inside the sunlit apartment.

Dawit has left the window to the terrace open, and the younger one strides across the living room and exclaims about the view, as though he has already taken over the apartment. The older one calls him to order with a discreet clearing of the throat, standing by the sofa, which Dawit has folded up neatly. The man fusses with his French cuffs with their gold cuff links. Then they sit down, without being asked, side by side on the gray two-seated sofa, where Dawit has sat beside Enrico. The older man motions to Dawit to sit in the straight-backed leather chair opposite them, his back to the view. "What can I do for you?" Dawit asks politely, drawing himself up and buttoning his jacket, trying to maintain some semblance of calm and dignity.

"You speak very good Italian." The young one seems surprised by this ability, though how they planned on conversing otherwise, Dawit cannot tell.

The young one asks him what he can tell them about M. "When did you last see her?" he asks.

Dawit says he's not sure he can give him the exact date but it was early September, when he dropped her at the airport. She had told him she was leaving for Switzerland. "She has a house in Switzerland," he says, looking at the older policeman, who is perusing papers he has in hand, as though not particularly interested in their conversation. From time to time he stifles a yawn, and his gaze is drawn toward the view out the window. His uninterest in the proceedings, though surely to his advantage, seems discourteous to Dawit, who tries to draw him into the conversation, addressing his answers to him.

"There seems to be no record of her on any of the flights during September," the young policeman says, pressing his lips together in an expression that might be either a sardonic smile or a snarl of disapproval. Dawit has him repeat what he has said, pretending not to understand.

"Really!" Dawit says, getting up, unable to sit still before them. He paces back and forth nervously. "How strange," he says. "*Molto strano!* Where could she have gone?"

The young one wants to know if he saw her through the gate at the airport, or if he just dropped her off at the terminal. Dawit says he did not take her inside, as she had told him she did not like lengthy good-byes and wanted to go in alone. Clearly he can hear M. telling him, "I don't like lingering good-byes." He sees her going up the steps to her suite, closing the wooden door on him. In the end, though, she had had a rather long, drawn-out departure.

As he speaks, feigning surprise and wonder, he has the

feeling that there is no point to all of this charade. Why is he telling all these absurd lies? What does it matter anymore?

"Did you happen to book her ticket for her or, perhaps, check on the time of her flight?" the older policeman asks, looking up from his papers and speaking for the first time, watching Dawit move back and forth in the small space. "Perhaps you'd be good enough, signore, to sit down. You are making me feel a bit seasick," he says with a hint of a smile. Dawit resumes his seat and wonders about the reference to the sea. Has anything been found? He looks from one to the other. He says M. made the arrangements herself, as she had her trip to Sassari that day. He had thought she was going to spend the night there, but she came back in the afternoon.

The young policeman wants to know what Dawit did after he had left her at the airport. Dawit hesitates, listening to the sound of the traffic in the street. Should he give them Enrico's name? Doing so would probably save his own life. Will Enrico really vouch for him as he said he would? What might he actually say?

Dawit says, deliberately avoiding their gaze, that he had met a friend in a bar, and they had spent the night together. The young one wants to know how to contact his friend. Dawit hesitates again. He keeps hearing Enrico's long, low moan, his cry to his God for mercy. He hears him say, "Who are we to decide?" *Indeed.* He says he would rather not give them this information. It might be compromising for his friend. He looks at the older man, who is watching him carefully now. "You do understand, don't you?" he says, appealing to the older man.

"Why is that?" the young man says with a hint of irony in

his voice, stretching his long legs out before him casually and fingering his bushy black mustache.

Dawit studies the carpet and asks if they can be discreet. His friend is a married man, he explains, looking down at the pattern in the carpet where he and Enrico lay together in vain. He adds that his friend is from the nobility and the wife is from a prominent family. He doesn't want to cause a scandal or any trouble in the marriage.

The younger policeman looks at the older, as if for guidance on this delicate point. There is a hint of a smirk on the younger one's face, probably thinking, *un frocio*. The older man just stares at Dawit. There is a moment of silence before the older one says slowly, "I understand fully. We will be as discreet as possible, but this information is important to us."

Dawit provides Enrico's name, and they look at each other again. "*L'architetto?*" the older one asks, raising his eyebrows, opening wide his dark eyes. Perhaps he even knows him, Dawit thinks. He nods his head.

Now the older policeman puts down his papers altogether and turns toward Dawit. He wants to know what his relationship is exactly with M. How did he meet her?

Dawit tells his story truthfully and in some detail. He directs his confession to the older man, speaking at some length and with considerable frankness of his life in Paris, his poverty, and his inability to find work, prior to the meeting in the café. He thinks he may be saying too much, that the policeman probably does not want to hear about all of this, about his friend Asfa and his poor wife, Eleni, and their generosity to those in need. Absurdly he even speaks of little Takla, and as he does so he longs to be with his friends, with people he knows, people who would not judge him whatever he did. He cannot stop himself from speaking of them at length and at the same time he wonders if he will ever see them again.

He tells the policeman he has worked as a secretary to M. through the summer. He helps her with her correspondence and edits her manuscripts, he can truthfully say. "She has been so good to me. I am very grateful," he says, looking from the older one to the younger. "I hope she's not in any trouble?"

The young policeman wants to know if M. seemed different in any way the last day they were together. "Do you think she might have been depressed?" he wants to know.

Dawit says it's possible, and certainly she seemed tired. He thinks of her gray skin, her greasy hair, the fetid breath. He thinks of her saying she was exhausted. She was worn out, he thinks, worn out with loving him. Her obsession with him had gradually worn her down. He tells them she had said she was planning to do a reading but felt too tired to go through with it and left. She has recently completed a new book, which he has helped her edit.

"Had she been drinking when you left her? She's a drinker, is she not?" the older one asks. Apparently he has done his homework.

Again Dawit hesitates, as if reluctant to speak ill of his friend, but then concedes, "She is rather a heavy drinker and is used to drinking several vodkas most evenings. But if she had drunk more than usual, I wouldn't have let her go," he says.

The young one looks at the older for a second, an inquiry in his eyes, raising his eyebrows. The older policeman tells

Dawit they would be glad if he would stay on in Rome for a while, in case they need to question him further. "Would it be possible for you to stay on for a while at this address?" he asks courteously, getting up and striding around the room. For now, that is all they need from him. Dawit feels a wild, violent joy at his words. They are not going to arrest him, or at least not immediately. Apparently they have no conclusive evidence of his role in this crime. Perhaps they have no indication that there has been a crime at all. No traces of M.'s body, he surmises, must have been discovered. It must still be lying somewhere in the depths of the bay, disintegrating slowly. The bay has kept his secret.

He says he will be happy to answer any additional questions they might have. He will stay on as long as necessary. He hopes they are able to find M. He is worried about her.

"I think you might have reason to be worried," the older policeman says, giving Dawit a curious glance as he goes out the door.

XXXVII

DAWIT IS ABOUT TO TELEPHONE GUSTAVE WHEN THE PHONE rings. He picks it up immediately, hoping it might be Enrico, but it is a journalist who wants an interview. He declines. Almost immediately the phone rings again. And again he snatches it up with hope. This time it is a woman who wants to invite him to dinner at her villa, the Contessa Bellini. Does everyone in Rome know where he is staying? How have they tracked him down?

She says she is an old friend of M.'s and has heard he is staying in Rome. She would be overjoyed if she could entice him to come. She is giving a big party—all of Roman society will be there, and they would be so grateful if he could come.

"You are—am I right? An Ethiopian *prince*?" she gushes.

"Not quite. My father's title was *ras*, which is really more equivalent to a duke, I think you might say." He laughs modestly. He thinks of his sophisticated father, part of the old aristocracy, not generally favored by the Emperor, who, like Napoleon, preferred to create his own coterie of nobles whom he believed would be more loyal to him. Still, his father had managed to keep his position at court due to his fierce loyalty, his wit, and his intelligence. What would he have had to say about his son now?

He is about to decline this invitation, which fills him with horror, when he realizes that if all of Roman society is coming, Enrico might very well be invited, too. He decides, despite his reluctance to face a crowd of curious strangers, to accept. Perhaps, too, it might be wise to mingle in society as much as possible.

The contessa gushes with joy at the thought of meeting him. She cannot wait to hear what he has to say about M. They are all *dying* with curiosity. Again, Dawit thinks how little anyone really seems to care that M. has vanished. All they want is gossip. He dares to ask how she tracked *him* down.

"Ah, we Romans have our sources of information," she says, laughing, and promises to send a car to pick him up and bring him to her villa on the outskirts of Rome. "You'll see, it is a wonderful old *cinquecento* house," she says.

He has only just put down the telephone when Gustave calls. Dawit tells him the police have paid him a visit. "How did it go?" Gustave asks.

"I don't know," Dawit can truthfully say.

Gustave returns to the topic of the book, which he is rushing out, as all of this publicity will be excellent for the sales. "You'll have to come back to Paris in November when the book appears. I want you to do some publicity for us," Gustave says.

"Me, publicity?" Dawit says, bewildered.

"You'll be perfect, I know. People will flock to see you, believe me." He adds, "I'll find you a place to stay, and we'll pay your expenses, so don't worry about any of that."

Dawit tells him about his invitation to the Roman party.

He laughs at the irony of it all and says, "I seem to be in great demand."

"Good, good. Don't hug the walls. Go out, talk about M., the new book," Gustave says and tells him to enjoy himself, too. No doubt all the hostesses in Rome will be after him. "Watch out! The women will eat you alive," Gustave says and chuckles. Dawit wonders what Gustave knows or suspects about his sex life.

Whatever that is, Gustave does indeed turn out to be correct. Dawit is in great demand, invited everywhere, photographed in the elegant clothes M. had pressed on him, standing smiling broadly on the arms of various society hostesses. His photo is, as he had feared, all over the tabloids, but not with the caption he had feared. How he would have loved all this attention only a few months ago, yet now, with his secret fear of disclosure, it fills him with terror. Journalists hound him, delighted with his story, his photogenic face, his slim form, his elegance, his excellent Italian. They call him the Prince from Abyssinia, the new Rasselas, who speaks perfect French, English, and Italian. When he tries to correct the error with his title, they simply say, "*Non fa niente, principe.*" They go on calling him "prince," which makes a better story. The Italians seem to have a loose concept of titles. People are whatever they want them to be. Everyone is *dottore* or something of that kind.

Everywhere he goes, Dawit looks only for Enrico in the crowd, but there is no sign of him. Perhaps he has left town. He never calls Dawit or leaves a message on the answering machine, and Dawit does not dare to call him. He hunts for him in the streets, thinking again and again that he has caught a glimpse of him disappearing down the street. He presumes the family lives somewhere nearby. He searches for the name in the telephone book but doesn't find it. He attends party after party, hoping to find him there. He is increasingly mobbed by Roman society. Everyone wants to know him, to say they have met him, to shake his hand. They want to know about M. What does he think? Where might she be? Might she have taken her life, or is she just hiding out somewhere like Salinger? Or might she actually have been murdered? Their eyes brighten with the thrill of the thought.

He is obliged to stand in crowded, ancient rooms, glass in hand, and talk about M. Everyone wants to know about her life, her habits, what his relationship was with her. Obviously they assume he was her lover. Forced to talk about her, he makes up a story as he goes along. He sings her praises, says he considers her a great writer, as indeed he once did. He says he is certain that her new book will stun them all. It is the best thing she has ever done, he maintains, echoing Gustave's words. He is sure she is somewhere, perhaps even back in Africa where she grew up, enjoying the landscape she loved. He is certain she must be amused by all the interest in her disappearance, her new book. Indeed, he does feel she is close to him, watching him, not so amused.

While he talks he thinks of her lying in the Bay of Foxes, something no living soul knows and probably will never know. He has two lives: one surrounded by an increasingly large and enthusiastic public and filled with falsehood, and another life running like an underground stream in secret. Everything that he really cares about—M.'s death, Enrico, his friends in Paris, his dead parents—all this he never speaks of, keeps hidden from others. He is cloaked in lies and begins to see others in the same light, thinking that they, too, must hide what is real.

He stands among the elegant people in the great, high-ceilinged halls of the Roman villas, looking out French windows at the cypress trees in the gardens, the moonlit stone paths. He thinks of his home and longs for his family. He feels more alone than he has ever done in his life.

As the autumn days go by, he is convinced that Enrico must indeed have confirmed his alibi, as the police have left him alone. This act of generosity saddens him further. He has underestimated his friend, who has stood by him gallantly. Why had he not gone to him immediately when M. had thrown him out? Would Enrico have been able to help him to find work, papers, enough money to support himself?

His allowance continues to be transferred to his account, and as he pays no rent and is invited for most of his meals, he has no financial worries. Even his tourist visa is easily extended with the help of his new and influential acquaintances. He lingers on, still hoping Enrico will come to him.

He continues to rise early and run barefoot in the streets of Rome. He runs around the Circus Maximus. Then he takes up his pen, the one M. had given him, and writes the story of his own life: about his childhood, Solo, the escapades in the hills around Harar. He writes about the Emperor, the revolution, his days in prison. He awaits a word from Enrico but it does not come.

XXXVIII

In November, the police telephone to tell him he is free to leave when he wishes. They have not turned up any trace of M. As so often happens with missing persons, there are no clues to her whereabouts, the inspector tells him. Dawit says nothing, thinking of the body lying silently in the depths of the sea. The Bay of Foxes has kept his secrets for him. He is free to go on with his life, to leave Rome, Italy, behind.

He phones Gustave, who is delighted with the good news and promises to send a ticket. "You might as well stay in M.'s apartment on the Rue Guynemer," he says. He tells him the apartment is empty, that it will take years before anyone can lay a claim to it. Dawit hesitates, thinking of those empty rooms he knows so well.

"Do you have the keys?" Gustave asks.

"I do, but . . ." Dawit says. He is reluctant to walk back into his past but does not know how to say this to him. Finally, he says nothing. Instead he tells him he has written his story. His book is finished.

"Wonderful news! Bring it with you. I can't wait to read it," Gustave says.

Dawit wonders what the editor will think when he does. "I'll be there in a few days and I'll bring you the book," he says.

On the day he leaves Rome, he packs his bag, tidies the flat, leaving things exactly as he had found them. He sits at the small fold-down desk against the wall, trying to compose a note for Enrico. "I owe you my life, which no longer has any meaning without you," he finally writes. He puts the note in a closed envelope and props it up on the counter by the telephone. He hopes Enrico will find it and read it, and perhaps one day respond. He takes a last look out the window at the Spanish Steps, then closes it, wipes off the counter in the kitchen, and leaves, putting the key under the mat as Enrico had asked him to do.

Gustave has sent him a business-class ticket on Air France and told him to take a taxi and charge it to the publishing house. Dawit looks out the window of the car at the streets of Rome that Enrico had promised to show him. They had never walked together to visit his favorite places, the parks and monuments, the Forum. Dawit feels grateful for the welcome the Italians gave him, grateful for the beauty and abundance of this country, and grateful to the couple in Sardinia, who must have spoken well of him to the police. He senses he will never return, that he is definitively saying good-bye to Enrico and to M.

When he arrives in Paris, it is after nine o'clock at night. The lights that flash by him outside the taxi window sadden him, but he reminds himself he will be able to call Asfa now, and that he will have a place to offer him where he might be able to stay with his family, at least for a while.

When he arrives at the elegant sandstone building in the Latin Quarter, he presses the brass bell as he did the first time.

As poor and hungry as he was that day, his heart was lighter and more hopeful than it feels now, for all his elegant clothes.

He knocks on the concierge's glass door, though he has the key. Maria greets him effusively, in her narrow loge, the smells of stew cooking in the air. She tells him she's so glad he has come back. "What news from madame?" she asks. He shakes his head and says he has none. "You must see my baby," she says in response and goes into her bedroom, brings out a bundle of white blankets, where a small dark face peeks out at him. "A boy," she says proudly. The child, wrapped up tightly in a thick blanket, is, to his surprise, dark-skinned, the hair a dark fuzz on the top of his head. "His father came from Africa," Maria explains, smiling at Dawit and putting the baby in his arms. He kisses the baby on both his plump cheeks. "He is beautiful, beautiful!" Dawit tells Maria, though the baby is quite plain as far as he can see. "Where is his father?" he asks with the child in his arms. She shakes her head, shrugs, and says sadly she doesn't know. Dawit sighs and holds the warm little body against his own. How well nature does its work, he thinks, feeling the child's warmth. It takes only a moment to fall in love with a baby, he thinks as he gives him back to Maria and takes out his wallet and pulls out all the money he has in it to give to her. She protests, "*Non, non, monsieur!*" He tells her to buy something nice for the baby. She says, "I'm so glad you are back. Will you stay with us for a while, monsieur?"

"Perhaps not very long, I'm afraid, and you must call me Dawit," he says.

Then Maria warns him that there is someone upstairs

waiting for him. For a moment he is startled, afraid M. will materialize as she did on that first day, with her distant expression, her blue jeans, the blue scarf tied prophetically around the long, arrogant neck. "Who is it?" he asks.

"A surprise," Maria says and smiles at him mysteriously. He presumes it must be Gustave. He will have to give him his book tonight. There will be no delay.

He takes the small caged elevator upstairs to delay his entrance, at least, and stands before the door, as he did that first day. He hesitates to use his key and decides to ring the bell instead. The door opens quickly, as though he were expected, and to his surprise it is not Gustave at all, but his wife, Simone. She is laughing and smiling as she welcomes him back, her white, even teeth glistening. She kisses him warmly on both cheeks. "Welcome! I'm so glad you are back," she murmurs. She wears a low-cut pink dress with frills on the shoulders and smells of a pungent perfume. Seeing his surprise as he enters the hall, she says she and Gustave thought he might prefer a little company on his first night back here in the empty apartment. What can he tell the poor woman? He says nothing, just looking around the elegant hall, the living room, with the low lamps lit.

"I have had the concierge tidy up and put some flowers in the vases for you," she says brightly, her cheerful French voice grating to his ears. He doesn't know how to respond. Trying to be polite, he tells her it was kind of them both to think of him. All he wants is for her to leave him alone. He strides away from her, murmuring something about the bathroom, going once again through the large rooms, the salon with its fireplace, where Simone has had a fire laid, the study with all

M.'s books, where he worked so hard for her. He goes down the corridor to his little bedroom at the end. Simone follows him like a shadow, as he once followed M. through this apartment. She stops at the door to his bedroom and watches him throw his suitcase onto the bed.

"You could sleep in the big bedroom now," she says, smiling suggestively.

"That's not necessary," he says, looking at her. "This is quite enough space for one."

She leans against the jamb of the door and asks him if his voyage was good. She says she has some dinner waiting for him. She will wait for him in the salon, while he freshens up. He listens to the click-clack of her high heels as she goes down the corridor. He is tempted just to throw himself down on the bed and sleep as he did that first day he came here, but he feels obliged to say something to Simone. She is waiting for him. He relieves himself, washes his hands, and gulps down a glass of water from the small basin in the corridor.

When he returns to the salon, Simone sits before the fire, her legs crossed, her sling-backed shoe dangling from her toes, sipping a glass of white wine. She looks up and says, "Ah, there you are, darling, do come and sit beside me, will you? Have some wine," and she pats the sofa at her side. But he stands at the French windows, looking out into the gardens, surveying the scene. At this season the trees have lost their leaves, and he can see the Panthéon through the dark tangle of branches, visible across the park, lit up in the dim light.

"You have had an anxious time, I hear. I do hope you will be happy again here," Simone says, getting up and coming over to him. She stands beside him, smiling, and puts her hand gently on his arm. She has prepared a little supper for them, she says, and if he does not mind she will share it with him.

He looks down at her and hesitates. He remembers that moment when M. had asked him to share a meal with her on his first night in her home. What would have happened if he had refused? This time he does just that. He tells Simone he is not feeling very well. He doesn't think he can eat. He needs to lie down. Indeed, he does not feel well. He is giddy, as though he is standing on a ship, the floor tilting under him. "So many terrible things have happened," he says, looking at her.

She draws herself up, purses her lips, and stares at him with her deep blue eyes. "So I have heard. As you prefer," she says coldly.

"Before you go, though, you must take my book for Gustave," he says and turns from her to fetch it. "I think he will find it interesting," he says as he thrusts it into her hands.

"You want me to take this now?" she asks, looking down at his pages with some distaste. "Surely it could wait a day or two? There's no rush, is there? You could, perhaps, bring it over one day next week yourself to the office?"

He hesitates for only a moment. "I think it's better you take it now, so that I don't change my mind," he says with a smile. She looks at him for a moment, then shrugs her smooth shoulders in her pink dress. He leads her to the door, helps her into her soft cashmere coat, and almost thrusts her forth onto the landing with his book in her reluctant hands. "Give it to Gustave. I think he'll be pleased," he says to her back as she presses the button for the elevator.

Then he goes into the living room and picks up the phone.

He calls Asfa at the hotel where he works and waits for someone to find him. He tells him he must come over tomorrow. He has space for him and his family, at least for a while. They must all come. He has written a book, and now, with the money, he is in a position to reciprocate.

"You wrote a book?" Asfa says. "That's wonderful."

"Yes, and you are in it. We are all in it, all the Africans, the French, and the Italians, too. It's called *The Bay of Foxes*."

Acknowledgments

Though this book is fiction and its characters fictional I would like to acknowledge the debt I owe these writers whose books were of great help to me:

Marguerite Duras and her biographers
Nega Mezlekia
Gaitachew Bekele
John H. Spencer
Kapuscinski
Haile Selassie
Dinaw Mengestu

And particularly Maaza Mengiste who was generous enough to read and comment on my text.

My thanks go to my colleagues at Bennington and Princeton for their support and encouragement and particularly Joyce Carol Oates, Edmund White, Amy Hempel, and Susanna Moore.

As always I thank my family: my three loving daughters, discerning readers and great generous hearts.

And my husband Bill for once again editing these pages with such diligence.

For the continuing support of my publisher at Penguin Books, Kathryn Court, I am most grateful.

A PENGUIN READERS GUIDE TO

THE BAY OF FOXES

Sheila Kohler

An Introduction to
The Bay of Foxes

The pampered son of Ethiopian aristocrats, Dawit is now an illegal immigrant living in Paris. Although he is finally safe from the revolutionaries who dethroned the emperor and killed both his parents, Dawit lives in poverty and constantly fears deportation. "He feels he has become invisible" (p. 7). Then a chance meeting offers him the opportunity to alter his destiny once more. While nursing a solitary espresso in a café, Dawit sees the famous author M. "With a thrill he recognizes the ethereal presence of a celebrity whom he sincerely admires" (p. 3). Much to his astonishment, Dawit realizes that M. is looking back at him.

As he already knows, the much older white woman also grew up in Africa, and many of her best-selling novels draw upon the events of her disreputable youth, including her passionate affair with a wealthy Somali landlord. Summoning Dawit to her table, M. tells him that he resembles this "lost lover" (p. 13). Even emaciated and in tattered clothes, Dawit is beautiful, and M. takes note of his elite education and courtly manners. They discuss Africa and their respective lives. "But he can see that she wants more from him than recollections of a shared past" (p. 13). At the end of their conversation, M. invites him to move into her apartment.

When the appointed day arrives, Dawit nervously sets off for his new patron's luxurious apartment. He is relieved that she remembers her invitation. Yet he also "wonders who inhabited this room before him, and why she had asked him to come three days after they had met" (p. 31). The two fall into a happy routine. Dawit becomes M.'s secretary and the first reader of her new work. An excellent mimic, he also takes over her correspondence and telephone conversations. When they dine with her editor, she boasts, "Who would have guessed what a dark gem I found in a café? A brown diamond" (p. 59).

Dawit's frail body begins to recover from the brutalities of his imprisonment and subsequent flight from Ethiopia. M. generously opens her elegant wardrobe of Italian suits and silks to Dawit, whose height and build are identical to hers, calling him her "very young and dark double" (p. 41). As Dawit's health returns, his gratitude toward M. grows peppered with contempt, until summer arrives and they travel to her Sardinian villa beside the Bay of Foxes. There, the glorious beauty of the Mediterranean renews his affection for M., but it also awakens his own long-buried sexuality—and his yearnings for freedom.

A stunning accomplishment by an internationally acclaimed author at the top of her game, Sheila Kohler's *The Bay of Foxes* explores issues of race, colonialism, and sexual politics in a chilling tale that deftly intertwines the events of Dawit's tragic past with his increasingly complicated present.

ABOUT SHEILA KOHLER

Sheila Kohler was born in Johannesburg, South Africa. She later lived in Paris for fifteen years. In 1981, she moved to the United States and earned an MFA in writing at Columbia University. She currently teaches at Princeton University and Bennington College. *The Bay of Foxes* is her twelfth work of fiction. She has been published in nine countries and now resides in New York City.

A CONVERSATION WITH SHEILA KOHLER

You've said that M. is loosely based upon Marguerite Duras. Was there a specific incident in her life that inspired The Bay of Foxes?

Not really one specific event, though I did remember that her partner, at some point in her life, was an Asian and that, of course, she spent her childhood in Vietnam. I transposed this to Africa, which is where I was born.

When Dawit first meets M., he is already an admirer of "her spare, concentrated prose, her brief, evocative novels" (p. 10). While this description certainly applies to the work of Marguerite Duras, it could also be said of your own. And while the main biographical details are Duras's, certain elements—the African upbringing and the position

*at a prestigious American university—are more evocative of your life
than hers. Was there any point in particular in plotting or writing
this novel where you found yourself merging with Duras?*

I suppose all characters lie in a "middle distance" somewhere
between the author and the character created on the page. I was
not aware at any point of writing about my own life, but of
course there are always elements of that in everything we invent.

*Have you spent much time in Ethiopia? How did you come to choose
that country as Dawit's homeland?*

No, I have never been to Ethiopia. I think I chose it because of its
history, its strong fight for independence, and its avoidance to a
large extent of a long history of colonialism. I admire many of the
young Ethiopian writers today who have brought the country to
life for me, as well as the historians who have recorded the reign
of Haile Selassie.

Midway through The Bay of Foxes, *Enrico visits Dawit at
M.'s villa, bringing "an Italian translation of a book by Patricia
Highsmith" (p. 114). Did you always intend for Dawit's path to echo
that of Highsmith's infamous character, Ripley?*

No, not at the start, though I'm an admirer of her work, but once
I realized there were echoes I wanted to acknowledge that. The
problem of identity has always been one that has interested me.
I remember as a teenager thinking, "Who shall I be? Melanie or
Scarlett O'Hara!"

When Dawit first moves in with M., he thinks, "Writers are like vultures, picking over the tragedies of other lives" (p. 13). Does this idea resonate with you in your own work?

Yes, I'm afraid so. We use our tragedies and sometimes the sufferings of others on the page. I hope, though, that we act as well as witnesses, reminding people of what has come before so that it will not be repeated.

Dawit tells M. that Haile Selassie was smothered with one of the same pillows used to elevate his feet from the ground. Is this true?

I don't think it is known exactly how Haile Selassie died, but the detail about the pillow for his feet is documented.

Although Dawit's character is sometimes in question, the novel's sympathies appear to lie with him. Is his "overthrow" of M., his oppressor, meant to mirror—and perhaps justify—the rebellion that dethroned Haile Selassie and killed Dawit's own parents?

I didn't think of it in those terms, but perhaps you are right. Certainly my sympathies were with him and with immigrants in similar situations who face such loneliness and loss in trying to establish new lives, though the older writer is also part of my story as you suggested.

You've lived in the United States since 1981. In what ways has living here affected your work?

America has been a place of possibilities for me. I'm very grateful for all the avenues that have opened up to me here in the publishing world as well as in academia. I have been very fortunate in the people I have met and those who have guided and helped me so generously.

What are you working on now?

A book on Freud and the Dora case. The title is *Dora's Freud*.

QUESTIONS FOR DISCUSSION

1. Dawit arrives at M.'s apartment with "a copy of Baudelaire's *Fleurs du mal*; Marguerite Duras's short stories, *Whole Days in the Trees*; and Dostoyevsky's *Crime and Punishment*" (p. 31). Why does Kohler include this detail?

2. Dawit condemns M. as a racist and "[l]ike all colonizers . . . ultimately the dupe" (p. 54). How do the events of the novel support or disprove his feelings?

3. Why didn't Michelino and Adrianna tell the police about M.'s sudden "departure"?

4. "These French intellectuals, for all their fancy talk, think about nothing but money in the end" (p. 186). Is Gustave more interested in profiting from M.'s final book or in her safe return? Does he suspect the truth?

5. Should Dawit pay for his crime or has he already?

6. *The Bay of Foxes* reverses the traditional alignment of gender and power, putting Dawit at the mercy of M., a powerful female. How—if at all—did this affect your reading of the novel?

7. What does the unexpected appearance of Maria's fatherless half-African baby add to the story?

8. How closely do you think Kohler's *The Bay of Foxes* resembles the book of the same name that Dawit wrote? Would you trust Simone to deliver the manuscript to Gustave?

9. Have you read Marguerite Duras? If so, how would you compare her writing to Sheila Kohler's? How does being an expatriate inform each writer's work?

To access Penguin Readers Guides online, visit the Penguin Group (USA) Web site at www.penguin.com.

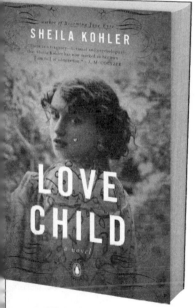

AVAILABLE FROM PENGUIN

Becoming Jane Eyre
A Novel

ISBN 978-0-14-311597-7

In a cold parsonage on the gloomy Yorkshire Moors, a family seems cursed with disaster: a mother and two children dead, a father sick and without fortune, a son destroyed by alcohol and opiates. And three strong, intelligent young women, reduced to poverty and spinsterhood, with nothing to save them from their fate. Nothing, that is, except for their incredible literary talent. So unfolds the remarkable story of the Brontë sisters, with Charlotte and the writing of *Jane Eyre* at its center.

PENGUIN
BOOKS